OMEGA REMEMBERED

BOOK TWO OF THE NORTHERN LODGE PACK SERIES

SUSI HAWKE

AN M/PREG PARANORMAL ROMANCE

Cover Art Designed by Cosmic Letterz

What happens when your fated mate is also your natural predator?

Get your FREE copy of The Rabbit Chase:

https://dl.bookfunnel.com/vfk1sa9pu3

Would you like to get updates about future releases? Sign up for my newsletter:

The Hawke's Nest
http://eepurl.com/cWBy9T

Twitter:
https://twitter.com/SusiHawkeAuthor

Facebook:
https://www.facebook.com/SusiHawkeAuthor

ALSO BY SUSI HAWKE

Northern Lodge Pack Series

Omega Stolen: Book 1

Omega Remembered: Book 2

Omega Healed: Book 3

Omega Shared: Book 4

Omega Matured: Book 5

Omega Accepted: Book 6

Omega Grown: Book 7

Northern Pines Den Series

Alpha's Heart: Book 1

Alpha's Mates: Book 2

Alpha's Strength: Book 3

Alpha's Wolf: Book 4

Alpha's Redemption: Book 5

Alpha's Solstice: Book 6

Blood Legacy Chronicles

Alpha's Dream: Book 1

Non-Shifter Contemporary Mpreg

Pumpkin Spiced Omega: The Hollydale Omegas - Book 1

Cinnamon Spiced Omega: The Hollydale Omegas - Book 2

Peppermint Spiced Omega: The Hollydale Omegas - Book 3

CHAPTER 1

MICAH

Smiling down at the precious, crying little girl in the filthy travel crib, I knew that I had finally found her. I remembered my cousin Daniel's friends, Jenny and Jake, and this baby smelled like a mixture of Jenny and that of our former Alpha who had disappeared a few months ago.

It'd been rumored that he and Helga took off with all the money in our pack treasury, fleeing for parts unknown, but I knew the truth. My cousin had told me about the events of the day that Alpha Fremont had shown up and tried to take Jake down in a challenge on his own land. Of course, Jake had taken him out. It was his right as the Alpha to take down a challenger.

Our pack here was in shambles now, and people had fled right and left. The ones who stayed were the ones that were too lazy to get involved with helping to keep up our pack-lands, so the place was going downhill fast. I couldn't get out of here fast enough to suit me, but first, I'd sworn to find this child.

I'd finally found this beta, Stanley, holed up at this

crappy little cabin by the lake. He had been babysitting this pup, for some reason known only to the old Alpha. I would never have entrusted a baby to that man's care, but that was a moot point now.

Stanley was dead. I'd snapped his neck after he'd admitted to me that he hadn't fed the pup since yesterday, when I'd asked why she wouldn't stop crying. He'd claimed that he couldn't afford any more formula, and that Fremont should have been back long ago. He said that he hadn't signed on to watch a baby for this long. And yet, when I looked in the fridge, it was full of beer.

Basically, the rat bastard could afford to buy beer, but not to feed a baby? Yeah, he had to die, no question. I had snapped his neck in a rare moment of anger, and now I just needed to get this pup home to her uncle's pack up north.

I looked around for diapers, but there were none to be found. The poor girl was so covered with filth that her little legs and privates were bright red and covered with a painful looking rash. No wonder the tiny thing screamed so much. I picked her up and took her into the bathroom.

I cuddled her against me while the water ran into the tub, testing it with the skin of my inner wrist to make sure it wasn't too hot or cold. I carefully set her down in it, but she started screaming harder as soon as her butt hit the water.

"Oh, baby girl. I'm sorry it stings," I cooed at her, releasing a relaxing wave of alpha hormones to soothe her. "Let's get you cleaned up, I promise it will feel better when we do."

I made faces at her, getting her to calm down, even giggling a little, as I finished up and lifted her back out of the water. Pulling the plug, I let the water drain while I took her to the kitchen. I found a few paper towels left on an old roll in there, which I used to pat her dry as gently as I could.

After she was dry, I rummaged through the cupboards until I found an old box of cornstarch. Perfect! Turning her over my arm, with her little butt up in the air, I sprinkled some of the fine powder over her butt and legs. It was a little more awkward to get her front powdered, since I wasn't about to lay her down on any of the filthy surfaces in this hell hole, but I managed to get it done.

In lieu of a diaper, I carefully shrugged out of my shirt while juggling the baby too. Once I had it off, I carefully wrapped the make-shift diaper around her tiny body.

"Alright, girlfriend! You ready to get out of here? Are you? Do you want to leave this dump?" I cooed at her, as we walked back through the main room. I didn't see any of her stuff that was still clean enough to even have near her, so I just took the car-seat that I found by the front door and got out of there.

I laid the baby on the front seat, and went around to the backseat to install the safety seat. I called my cousin, Daniel, while I fastened it into the car. By the time he answered, I was already reaching over the seat to grab the baby. After safely fastening her into the seat, I snapped a quick photo with my phone.

"Hello?"

"Hey, Danny-boy. It's me."

"Micah! Where are you? I thought you were joining us up here."

"I am, I'm leaving now actually. I just wanted to give you some good news for the Alpha. Also, I need a favor from you."

"What's going on?"

"Check your messages, I'm sending a text right now of a little princess that I just found being, and I use the word loosely, babysat by some beta prick named Stanley. But you should probably know that I had to kill him when I saw how he had treated her."

At Daniel's intake of breath and choked sob, I knew that I had done the right thing in sticking around until I found the baby. I only wish that I had found her sooner.

"What do you need, Micah. Name it. Just bring Erin home."

"Erin? That's her name, huh? Cool. All I need is some diapers, clothes, a blanket, and some diaper rash cream. Maybe a few toys? I dunno. It's gonna be long trip. Plus, I really don't know what she eats, so I'm really gonna need some help in that department too. The fucker told me that he hadn't even fed her since yesterday, so that part probably needs to happen quick."

"Do you need money? Or do you just not know what to buy? I don't get why you need my help for that stuff. I don't mind, I'm just confused."

"Daniel, take a good look at that picture I sent you. If I take this poor child into any stores, I'm going to have the humans calling CPS or some shit. She's filthy, for one thing. She has no clothes on, except for my shirt that I'm using as a temporary diaper. Oh, yeah, so add in that the naked baby is in the company of a shirtless man. Yeah, that will go over well. Anyway, her legs, ass, and girl parts are covered in red welts from a diaper rash to end all rashes, and her hair is matted to her head in places. This baby has been neglected to the point of abuse. I hate to tell you all that, but I need help if I'm going to get her quietly out of here, and home where she belongs with her uncle."

"Fuck. Did you say that you killed Stanley? Because if you didn't, then go back and snap his fucking neck right now for me."

"Done, dude. That was my first move."

"Righteous. Okay, head to Angela's, she has a kid about Erin's age, she should be able to hook you up. I'll call her now. If there's a problem, I'll call you back, but I'm sure she will help you out."

"Thanks, Daniel. I can't believe that I didn't think of Angie in the first place. Of course she'll help me out with the little princess here. Now, go and give your Alpha the good news. I know that you're probably dying to tell him."

"Ha! I will, but first I'm going to call Angela. Let's get Erin taken care of and fed before anything else."

"Perfect. Thanks, Daniel. Talk to you soon."

"Yep, thanks Micah. Love you, cousin."

"Love you too, cuz."

I closed Erin's door, but as I was walking around the car to get in the driver's seat, I saw the curtain move in a room I hadn't checked out while I was inside the cabin. Two little faces were peeking over the window sill in the dark room. If I hadn't been paying attention, I wouldn't even have seen them.

Unsure what to do with the baby, I decided that I really couldn't leave her alone in the car, even if we were in the middle of nowhere. I went back over and got her out of the car, whispering in her ear, "Why didn't you tell me you had friends in there, Princess?"

She gurgled up at me, a string of drool hanging from her plump little lip. I hadn't smelled any other wolves in the cabin, but I hadn't been exactly paying that close attention anyway, to be fair. I knew that I would've noticed if there had been another adult present though; our scents were stronger than those of little pups.

Even though I was pretty sure it was safe, I still carefully held Erin against my chest with my left hand as I crept back into the cabin. Stepping quietly through the filthy main room, I went over to the room off to the side that I'd ignored in my earlier wanderings.

Taking a deep breath, I grabbed the door knob and opened it quickly. The light from the main room flooded in through the open door, and there by the window, I saw two little kids huddled together. They were trembling with fear, their little arms wrapped around each other and looking up at me with eyes as wide as saucers.

Sending out a flood of calming pheromones, I knelt in the doorway and said: "Hey, I didn't know there were two pups in here. My name is Micah, what's your name?"

The older one, an adorable little girl, spoke up softly and said with the most fucking adorable little speech impediment: "My name Sawa. Dis Dywan. He my bwuva."

"Hi, Sara, and you too, Dylan," I said warmly. "How come you didn't come out and say hello before, when I was taking care of Erin?"

"Becoz Stanwee tode us to not weave da woom. Who Ehwin? Dat baby Natawee. Huh my sistuh."

"Oh, you guys call her Natalie? Well, her real name is Erin, that's what her mommy named her."

"You mean Hugga? Huh not owah mommy. Her da mean wady dat da mate to owah alfa daddy."

"No, baby girl, not Helga. You guys won't ever have to see her or your alpha daddy again. I came to take Erin home to live with her uncle. Why don't you guys show me where your shoes and coats are, and you can come with us. I know you want to be with your sister."

Sara looked at me hesitantly before answering. "Wot

'bout Stanwee? Him say no weave dis woom. We get in twubble."

"Don't worry about Stanley," I assured her. Realizing that I'd left his dead body lying out in the front room behind me, I quickly said: "Stanley is sleeping. We can go right now, and I promise that he won't ever bother you again. Okay?"

She and Dylan looked at each other, then over at Erin, who was happily gnawing her own little fist, still safely tucked against my chest.

"Otay, mistuh. We go wif you." Sara turned to Dylan and said, "Go get you swoos on, we go bye-bye wif da man."

Dylan scampered over to a bunk bed near the window, and crawled under it. A moment later, he popped back out with shoes that he quietly carried over to his sister. I watched as the tiny girl put shoes on her brother, before calmly going over to the same bed and retrieving her own.

With a choked voice, I asked, "Do you have coats?" Sara shook her head no, as she fought to shove her chubby little foot into a shoe that looked at least half a size too small.

I blinked back tears for these sweet angels, and asked another question. "What about more clothes or toys? We need to take whatever you have with us now, because we're never coming back here again."

Sara looked up at me. "Otay, mistuh man. I go get dem."

She crawled back under the bed, emerging a moment later with a little plastic bag emblazoned with the logo from a local liquor store. It didn't look to contain more than a few scraps of cloth, but I reached my hand out to take it from her anyway. She shook her head and held it firmly to her little chest, while also reaching her hand out to clasp hands with Dylan.

"Okay, angel. Let's just get you guys in my car then." I

stopped for a second, as I realized that I now needed two more car seats. "Hey, Sara. Do you and Dylan have seats for the car?"

"No, mistuh man, dere onwee one seat.. Alfa daddy say we haffa be woof pups fo da cah wides. You wan dat we swift to pups?"

I thought about it quickly, weighing the odds between two little ones being buckled for a few miles without a safety seat, versus having them shift only to find myself wrangling wolf pups. Yeah, neither option was good, but I definitely had to vote for option A.

"That's okay, Sara. Let's save our wolves for playtime, okay? I'll figure it out when we get you in the car."

Sara nodded her head, looking up at me with a serious expression in her big, brown eyes. I stood up, and said guiltily: "Um, let's walk out quietly, so we don't wake up Stanley."

She looked at me like she knew I was lying for some reason, but rather than call me out on it, she just calmly walked out ahead of me with her brother in tow. I grinned at the gumption of this tiny angel, and followed them over to the door that I'd left open on my way in.

I herded them down the porch and over to my car. I opened the back door and waved for them to get in. They scrambled in and climbed over to sit next to Erin's safety seat. I fastened Erin in, closing the door after I stepped away. After a quick walk around the car, I opened the door on the other side, and looked in at the two little ones who were staring up at me expectantly.

"Okay, guys. Here's what we're going to do," I said, thinking about the best way to do this. "This is really not safe, but it will have to work for tonight until I can get you all to safety. You two are going to wear a regular seat belt, and you're going to promise me to sit tall and still until we get where we're going, got it?" They nodded solemnly as I buckled the lap belts, cinching them as snugly as I could across the width of their little hips, fastening them in together.

I stood and closed the door, running a hand through my hair as I wondered what the hell I'd just gotten myself into, and so glad that I'd found them at the same time. I waved my fingertips at them, smiling to reassure them, as I pulled out my phone and called my cousin back. He answered on the first ring.

"Hey, Micah. You at Angela's already?"

"No, I actually am just now leaving. There was a complication."

"What kind of complication?" he asked in a worried tone.

"Don't freak out, Daniel, but it turns out that Erin has a couple of siblings. I caught them watching me through a window as I was about to leave earlier."

"Holy shit, are you serious, Micah? How old are they?"

"I don't know much about kids, but the girl is about three I would guess, and the boy is probably two-ish."

"And you have them in your custody?"

"Yep, and I'm about to take them all to Angie's right now. She can help get them all sorted out, and then I guess I'll be driving north with three little ones."

"Thanks, Micah. I appreciate what you're doing. Do we know where the other two came from?"

"Not a clue man, pretty sure they don't either. Maybe you should ask the omegas you have up there, one of them might be able to shed some light on the situation. Other than that, I don't know what to tell you. They definitely both smell like Fremont sired them, though, so maybe let

Seth and Maxx know. They may be the closest thing to family that these pups have left. I'll send a picture when I can, maybe it will help you guys to figure out where they came from."

"Okay, well, get those kids out of there, and I'll see what I can dig up. Talk to you soon, Micah. Oh, and before I forget? You made the Alpha's day. Jake has been in tears since I told him, he's that happy."

I smiled as I hung up the phone, glad that I'd done my part to help bring the little princess together with her family. I only hoped that I could do the same for the other two little angels. Getting in the car, I adjusted my mirror so I could keep an eye on the three little ones in the backseat.

I pulled out on the dirt road that led away from the cabin and said, "Okay, kiddies. Let's the road!"

CHAPTER 2

ARIES

Seth came in while I was cooking dinner, and sat down heavily on a stool at the counter. I walked over and set a mug of coffee down in front of the kind alpha. "What's up, Seth? You okay today?"

He looked at me and sighed. "Would you believe that Jenny wasn't the only omega that Fremont stole a baby from?"

I froze, my heart racing in my chest, as I frantically tried to breathe. "Why do you say that, Seth? How did you find out? Did they find them both?"

Seth's eyes narrowed thoughtfully, as he replied, "I said baby, singular, Aries. I didn't say that there were two. But as a matter of fact, Daniel's cousin found a little girl and boy being watched by Stanley at your old cabin when he went there on the hunt for Jenny's little Erin."

His words became garbled, as the room pressed in around me. I gasped for air as the world went fuzzy and I dropped to my knees. Seth quickly jumped up and raced around the counter to get to me.

"Aries! Breathe, man. It's okay, I'm right here, you're

safe." Seth breathed these words into my ear, as he wrapped his arms around me and pulled me up against his broad chest for a comforting hug. I trembled against him, as tears poured down my cheeks.

"What's going on in here?" I heard Daniel's voice calmly asking, as a flood of calming alpha pheromones filled the room.

"I think we don't have to look too far to solve the mystery of who Sara and Dylan's carrier is," Seth answered over my head. "I was just sharing with Aries what you told me about my little cousins, and he kinda freaked out here."

Daniel walked over and rested a big hand on top of my head. "Is that true, Aries? Could those be your pups?"

I bit back a sob and nodded my head against Seth's chest. "I think so. Or, I hope so anyway. I haven't seen either of them since they were born, I didn't even know if they were alive!"

I broke into full sobs then, my shoulders shaking as I cried. I felt a smaller pair of arms come around me from behind, and smelled Sy's familiar scent brush up against me.

"Come on, Seth," Sy said huskily. "Let's get Aries up and over to the table." Seth slid a hand under my legs and stood up, lifting me right along with him, while Sy slipped in front of us and pulled out a chair. Seth sat me down, and Sy immediately slid into the chair next to me and reached out for my hand.

I smiled sadly at my old friend. With Jenny gone, Sy was the only one left who truly knew what we had suffered from the old Alpha-pair of Fremont and Helga. Our own Alpha-pair came in right then, with Kai riding piggyback on Jake's broad back.

"Hey, Daniel," Kai chirped happily, "Did you tell Seth and Maxx about their little cousins yet?"

Daniel and Seth both looked up at him, and tilted their heads at me, as if to stop him from talking. Kai bumped Jake on the arm, saying, "Oops, let me down, baby. I need to check on my boys."

Alpha Jake looked at me with concern, letting out yet another wave of calmness into the air, while letting Kai slide down to the floor. Kai came over and wrapped his arms around my shoulder, resting his cheek against mine.

"I'm so sorry, Aries. I didn't know. I didn't even know you had ever even had a baby! Let alone two of them. Why didn't I know this? I feel like an asshat for not knowing."

I patted his hand distractedly, while Sy answered for me. "It was long before you came around, Kai. Aries was there longer than any of us. I got there right after the old Alpha-pair had taken his newborn son. It was dark days that we really don't talk about," he finished glumly.

Reaching over to rest my hand on his, I squeezed his hand that rested on the table in front of him. "Sy, it's only luck that we were rescued before Brianne was born. Don't feel guilty because you have your daughter and I didn't have my pups. Our circumstances are different, but the pain we share is the same. Neither of us asked to be fathers, you know that."

Turning his hand over to clasp mine, Sy looked back at me with tears in his eyes. "Yeah, but Brianne is worth all of the pain that I endured. I'm just so very happy that your babies have been found."

Alpha came around to sit near Daniel at the back of the table, pulling his phone out. "Aries," he said. "I came down here to show Seth and Maxx a picture of their cousins, because I had no idea who their other parent was before now. Here, look at this."

I took his outstretched phone and gasped with joy.

There, on the screen, were my babies! My little ones were so precious, with their big, brown eyes that were just my color and the black curls that I'd also had at their age.

Kai and Sy leaned over me, eagerly looking at the image on the phone. I couldn't trust myself to speak just yet, so I just sat there staring happily at the screen.

Seth spoke up and said, "Wow, I just realized something! Brianne, Erin, and Aries' pups are all half siblings. How great is it that they'll all be together now, with all of us here to love them?"

Sy and I shared a smile, as that sunk in. I'd been so busy staying away from little Brianne because of the deep sorrow that I felt at the loss of my own babies. I had honestly never realized that our pups were siblings.

"That's amazing, Sy! I almost want to run up to the nursery and kiss your baby right now, while I wait for mine to get here!"

He grinned happily."I have to restrain myself from running up and kissing her all the time anyway! I hate when she's sleeping and I can't cuddle her."

We all laughed, because as much as that was true, Sy was also a very cautious parent who tried really hard to not spoil his little one.

"Hey, Aries. What are the pups' names?" Kai asked me, as he walked around the table to sit on Alpha's lap.

I sighed heavily, and looked back down at the dear faces smiling up at me from the screen that I still held tightly in my hand. "I didn't name them. I knew I would probably never see them again, it just hurt too much, without also having named them. Jenny ached every moment after they took Erin. I tried to tell her not to name her, but you know how Jenny was."

Alpha smiled sadly, nodding in agreement. "Yeah,

Jenny would never have been able to refrain from naming her baby. But I understand your point."

"Do you know their names, Alpha?" I asked hesitantly, eager yet afraid to hear details about my children, until I actually held them in my arms.

Daniel answered. "The girl is called Sara, and your son is Dylan. My cousin believes them to be about two and three, is that about right?"

"Yes," I nodded, in a daze at hearing their names. "Sara will be four in a few weeks actually, and Dylan is two and a half."

"Damn," Seth breathed. "Aries, dude. I had no idea that you'd been held that long. I'm so sorry."

Waving a hand at him, I said, "Not your fault who your family was, Seth. You didn't ask for Helga to be your aunt or for the pair of them to have to take you and Maxx in after your parents died. Don't even worry, I hold no grudges against you, my friend."

He nodded miserably though, looking from me to Sy, and then down at the table in front of him. Poor Seth, he carried so much guilt that wasn't his to bear.

"Alpha," I asked, "may I text this photo to myself? I'm sure you don't want me to keep your phone all day."

He grinned and nodded his assent. "Of course! I should have thought of that myself."

I quickly forwarded the photo to my phone, and passed his back over after taking one last look at the chubby-cheeked little darlings. "Where are they now?" I asked Daniel. "Seth mentioned something about your cousin having found them, when he was looking for Jenny's baby? Are they on their way here now? I can't believe it took me so long to ask!"

Daniel smiled gently at me. "Yes, my cousin Micah will

be here with them in about two days, I think. He would have left already, but he needed help with them. Not to mention that Stanley hadn't been taking proper care of them, and they had no belongings to speak of at all. I don't want to upset you. I'll wait to share all the details until you've had a chance to see them for yourself."

I gasped. "I totally glossed over the fact that Stanley had them at the cabin. I was so overwhelmed when Seth mentioned my pups that I ignored the rest of what he was saying."

Kai and Sy looked sick when they heard who'd been watching the pups, and where he'd been keeping them. I pushed my horror aside, deciding to worry about that later. Right now, I would focus on the fact that they had been found.

Stanley was a beta wolf who had guarded the cabin full of omegas that our old Alpha Fremont, and his wife, Helga, had held captive there. He had kidnapped or bought all of us, with the intention of forcing us to breed him an alpha heir. He forced us each to mate with him when we went into heat, and his wife would stand there watching dispassionately while it happened.

If we got pregnant, our pups were taken away at birth, never to be seen by us again. Five of us were males, but there were also three females that had been there at one time or other. One of the girls died in childbirth, along with the baby. One ran away in the night when she had the chance, and we never knew what had happened to her. The third was Jenny, whose baby Erin it was that Micah had gone to rescue.

Jenny was the whole reason we'd all been saved from our captivity. Our new Alpha, Jake, was her twin brother. After she was kidnapped, he spent an entire year looking for her until he tracked her down. When he found her, he also found Kai, his fated-mate. He ended up bringing all of us with them when he and his pack of alpha buddies rescued her.

We all moved up here to this fabulous northern lodge owned by Jake's aunt, and we had formed our own pack with Jake as our Alpha. Unfortunately, Jenny had been killed four months ago, when Fremont and Helga had arrived to try and take us back.

Jake had killed Fremont, but Helga had taken Jenny out. Sy killed Helga right after, in a fit of revenge. It was a bad, bad day, but we were all slowly healing now. I was glad that Jake would have Jenny's daughter here now. It'd be like having a piece of his sister back. Fenris be thanked!

I got up to go put on a pot of tea, needing a little comfort now. Sy pushed me back down into my chair gently. "Sit. I'll go fix a cup of your damned tea. You've had a shock, so just chill and let us take care of you for once."

Kai nodded. "Yes, and I want to help with dinner. I know you've been giving me way too much slack because of the twins, but they're three months old now. It's time I help out again. Besides, I miss cooking!"

"But what about your pups?" I asked curiously.

Kai smacked Alpha across the chest with the back of his hand, saying: "They have another father! Besides..." He grinned. "Aunt Kat loves having time with them."

Alpha said, "And we could always bring them in here in the travel crib if I'm tied up, it's really not a problem."

"That's true," I agreed. I'd never had to worry about things like that before, since I hadn't been able to be around my own children. As if reading my mind, Daniel reached over and clapped a hand on my shoulder.

"Just think, Aries!" he said kindly. "This time next

week, you'll be the one needing to figure out the balancing of life and childcare."

"I know," I breathed, looking back at him in wonder. "Isn't that fabulous?"

"Only you," Sy laughed, as he set a cup of tea down in front of me, "would be over the moon about dealing with pups."

"Please," scoffed Kai, "like you aren't still that way with Brianne, she's almost six months old and you still hate to leave her in the nursery!"

Sy blushed while we grinned, knowing full well how attached he was to that gorgeous child of his. All of us were actually; we adored the babies that were starting to fill out our pack, and making us all a family. Even the big, bad alphas melted into puddles of goo when the babies were in the room. It was a problem how addictive those pups were. And soon, I would have my own here too! I couldn't wait.

CHAPTER 3

MICAH

I had planned to get right on the road the following morning, but once Angie had seen the three pups in my care, she had put her foot down. Little Erin had an ear infection apparently, and a low grade fever. This was in addition to that fucking awful rash she had, and teeth that she was cutting.

The older two needed to eat and rest after their trauma before going on a long road trip. Dylan still hadn't spoken a word. I wasn't sure if he was mute, shy, or just too traumatized to speak. For now, Sara spoke for both of them.

Angie couldn't understand a word that Sara said, leaving me to translate, since I had absolutely no problems knowing what she said. Sara was my little angel girl. The more time I spent with her, the more she had me wrapped around her little finger.

I had sent a photo of them to Daniel, after they'd had a proper bath and their hair washed. I was amazed by their bouncy curls, and constantly found myself playing with the pups' hair. It was a problem, how much these kids tugged at my heartstrings.

I'd never been around kids, or ever even thought about having pups of my own, but if I could? I would want ones just like these ones. They were simply perfect in every way. I couldn't put my finger on it, but they reminded me of someone. Something about their eyes spoke to my soul, I just for the life of me couldn't place what it was.

"Okay, Micah," Angie said, walking into the living room where I was finally relaxing while the kids were all napping. "I had an idea that I want to run by you."

I looked over at my old friend. The poor thing looked so frazzled, with her uncombed, brown waves thrown up in a ponytail and rings under eyes from being up last night with her own sick baby.

Shifters didn't usually get sick, but babies were still fragile and had weaker immune systems than we adults did, so they did get the occasional illness. They just thankfully passed faster than in human children. Erin was already healed after the two days we'd spent with Angie, and I had plans for us to hit the road before sunrise.

"What's up, buttercup?" I asked her with a teasing lilt.

Shaking her head, she went on: "I cannot, in good conscience, allow you to travel almost a thousand miles by yourself, with two young pups and a baby. That's insane."

"What else am I supposed to do, Angie? I need to get those pups home."

"I know, and like I said, I have an idea."

Quirking a brow, I leaned back into the sagging, brown couch and spread my arms out across its low back behind me. "Alright, run it by me then."

Coming over to sit next to me, she sat sideways, with her knees pushed up against my thigh. "Remember the Collins family, that lived down the street from Daniel's house when we were growing up?"

"Yeah, of course I do! We had some good times over there." I smiled, as I remembered the stunts I'd pulled with Tommy Collins when we'd been pups. "Hey, how is Tommy? I haven't seen him since I moved back from the city last year. But then, I haven't seen a lot of people."

Angie sighed and put a hand on my arm, "Sweetie, Tommy died last year. I thought you knew."

"What the hell? I had no idea! How? Fuck, Angie, he was our age!"

"I know, babe." She leaned back, propping her shoulder against my arm that was stretched out beside her. "He and his parents were killed instantly in a car accident, on their way to Zane's graduation."

"Oh, merciful Fenris! Are you kidding me? What happened to Zane?"

"Well, that's the whole point. He couldn't exactly stay alone in their family home, being an omega and all. His alpha cousin, Steve, sold the house and put the money into savings for Zane, and he's been living with Steve and his family since then."

I rubbed a hand over my face, trying to process all this information. "Poor Zane. If Steve is half as shitty as he was as a kid, then I feel sorry for the guy. Remember how that lazy little fucker used to make everyone else do everything while he just sat there? And how if anything happened, he was the first to snitch us out? What a prick. I mean, it's good he took Zane in? But, still. Poor Zane."

Angie grinned knowingly and said, "Exactly. And now he's mated with four pups, so he basically has Zane as a free, live-in manny for them. Zane needs an escape, and this is the perfect solution for you both."

I thought for a second, before I said: "And how does

Zane feel about going with me and three young pups for a thousand mile trip away from home?"

"I talked to him last night, and he was ecstatic at the idea. That is, if you think the pack up there will take him."

"Oh, I'm sure that's not a problem. Let me call Daniel right now, and work it out. And, knowing Steve? You might want to go take Zane to cash out his savings, before he tells Steve he's leaving. Steve is just petty enough to try and block him from it, if you don't."

"Good idea! I'll go grab Zane now, and you keep an ear out for the pups. Call my cell if you need me?"

"You got it, babe. If you want, have Zane pack his shit and bring him back with you. That way we can just leave from here in the morning."

"Ha! I bet he packed when he hung up with me last night! But I'll make sure we get his stuff and let him say good-bye to Steve. After we hit the bank, of course."

"Of course. Sounds good, I'll order us all pizza tonight. I think you need a break, baby girl."

Flashing her trademark dimples at me, Angie quietly slipped out and went to run her errand, while I called Daniel and talked to him about Zane. I already knew the pack would open their arms to the orphaned omega, but I still had to ask.

"Holy crap! You can't be Tommy's little pain in the ass brother," I teased when Zane came walking in behind Angie an hour later. The pups were all up from their nap. The older ones were playing quietly with blocks, while I had the two babies in the playpen with their own toys.

Zane blushed and gave me a sad half smile. "Hey,

Micah. You grew up kinda big yourself. I haven't seen you in what, ten years?"

"Something like that," I agreed. "I'm sorry to hear about your family, Zane. I would've been there for you, if I'd known. Tommy was family to me, you know?" I stood up to give him a hug, asking as I stretched out my arms, "How are you doing, kid? You okay?"

He nodded, and stepped into my hug. "I'm okay, Micah. It's been hard, but I'm getting there. It's kind of been a day by day, moment by moment type thing."

"I get that," Angie said from beside me. "That's pretty much the only way to get through the hard times. Moment by moment. Just stay strong, Zane. You'll get there. And remember, you can call or text me whenever you need a friend."

With one last pat on his back, I released Zane so he could step back and set down his bags. He looked around the room, taking in all the little ones.

"Wow, Angie! Your little dude has really grown since the last time I saw him," Zane commented while smiling down at her son, Rex. "And who's this little princess sitting next to you, Rexie?"

"Dat my sistuh. Huh name Ewin, not Natawee, otay?"

Zane grinned at Sara, before looking back at Angie and me for translation.

"Don't look at me, buddy." Angie laughed. "Micah here is the pup-whisperer and master translator."

I shrugged. "What's to translate? Sara just told you herself! That's her sister, Erin, not Natalie, in case you didn't know any better."

I ignored the amused snorts from the other adults in the room and squatted down to pup level. I held my arms out for my angel. She came running over and climbed on my back, wrapping her arms around my neck in a choke hold.

"This is Miss Sara, also known as my angel. And my little dude over here is Dylan." I held a hand up, palm outstretched. Dylan came running over to give me a high-five. Fuck, I seriously loved these kids already.

"It's nice to meet you, Sara and Dylan," Zane said, with all the seriousness that he could muster. "My name is Zane, and I'm going to be traveling with you to go live with your other daddy."

I did a mental facepalm at his innocent words, since I hadn't yet told Sara and Dylan about having a dad on the other end. I had only gotten a text the day before from Daniel about it. I probably should have told Angie that it was a secret for now, since she'd obviously spilled it to Zane.

I could feel the tension rising from Sara, as she squeezed my neck harder and hugged against me, saying petulantly, "Don' wanna nutter daddy. Mistah man my nutter daddy. Mistah man be me and Dywan nutter daddy. Don' need no mo daddy."

I reached around and swung Sara down to snuggle into the curve of my arm, while also crooking my finger in a "come here" motion to Dylan. He ran into the safety of my other arm.

Looking into their vulnerable little faces, I fought back tears as I said, "Hey, guys, it's okay. I'm not going anywhere! I'm going to be right there with you in our new home. Do you remember how some pups have mommies and some pups have daddies?"

They both nodded solemnly. "Well, just like Rex has a mommy that loves him and would miss him if he were gone, you two have a daddy that loves and misses you. He has been missing you both since you were littler than Erin. You will love your daddy, I promise."

"No." Sara insistently declared: "You da Nutter Daddy. We don' need no mo daddy. Jus you, Nutter Daddy."

Zane's red face looked like he was trying to decide whether to laugh or cry, but Angie just clapped me on the shoulder and said, "Okay, Nutter Daddy. You heard the girl, so let's leave it for now. Just sort it out up north, you know? But for now? How about we order some pizza and feed these chitluns?"

I hesitantly nodded my agreement, despite my misgivings. I loved these pups too much to make promises, implied or otherwise, only to take them back later. They had never had anyone to count on in their lives, and I was damned well not going to be yet another asshole adult to these precious babies.

After dinner, Angie settled the kids in the play area for a cartoon movie, while she took turns bathing each of them. While that was going on, Zane got the car loaded up for the trip, and I installed the three new safety seats that I'd purchased for the pups.

"Hey, Micah?"

"Yo, Zane, what's up?" I asked, as I fought with the tethering device that anchored this Fenris-damned contraption into the car. Ugh, and this was just the first one! I still had two more to go after this one.

"I just want to apologize for earlier. I didn't know that they didn't know about their carrier dad yet."

"Naw, don't sweat it, Zane. There's no way you could have known. This whole situation is tough, no getting around that. I'm just doing my best to keep the little ones calm, and make them feel safe until I can get them to their dad. They haven't had it easy, so I'm just trying to not to confuse them, you know? But it's okay, they'll adapt, kids are great that way. Or at least, that's what Angie tells me."

"That's true, kids are quite adaptable. Angie told me about the condition you found those pups in. They're lucky that you're the one who found them. Life is going to be so much better for them now. You might wanna watch out though, Micah. Because I think that they're already super attached to you."

"Yeah, I've noticed that. It's probably just because I'm the first person who's ever given a shit about them, ya know? It's cool though, they'll be with their real dad soon, and forget all about *Mistuh Man*." Even as I said this, I couldn't help but feel a pang of loss.

"You sure about that, *Nutter Daddy*? Because from where I'm standing, those pups aren't the only ones that are already super attached."

"I'm sure, Zane," I said abruptly. I was super attached to ending this conversation, was what I was thinking. "Let's just get this shit done, so we can hit the road in the morning. I need to get some shut eye since I'm the only driver."

"Okay, Micah. Sorry if I'm overstepping, I just don't want to see you or those little guys getting hurt when this is all over."

"I know, man," I sighed, as I hooked the next safety seat into the car. "I don't mean to snarl at you. It just kills me to see how those pups suffered, and yet they still shine like little beacons of joy. And those eyes of theirs? Like pools of melted chocolate. Gets me every time, I gotta admit."

I couldn't figure out what was niggling the back of my mind about those sparkling little pairs of eyes, but it was *something*. I just couldn't put my finger on what it was. We finished up our task, and went back inside.

About an hour before sunrise, I gave Angie one last hug good-bye after she helped me and Zane to load the three sleeping pups into the car and get them safely fastened into their seats.

"Thanks, girl," I said gruffly, holding her hands in mine and touching my forehead to hers. "If things ever get too hard down here, you know that Daniel and Jake will welcome you into the new pack up north. Just say the word, and I'll come pick you up myself, if you don't wanna make the trip on your own."

"I know, babe." Angie smiled softly. "I have really enjoyed having you and the wee ones here with me and Rex these past few days. The house is going to be so quiet now, I might just have to take you up on that offer at some point."

"Well, it's a standing offer, so just let me know. You're always going to be pack to me, part of my family, you know?"

"I know. Now, shut up and get out of here, before you make me cry, Micah Knight!"

My old friend was already blinking back tears. I smirked knowingly at her before I leaned in and gave her one more quick hug. I let her go and slipped around to take my spot behind the wheel, while Angie and Zane said their own goodbyes.

A few minutes later, we were finally on the road at last. I blew out a breath of relief to know that we were finally on our way to a new life, a new pack, and a most importantly, a new start for the three little ones currently in my care.

CHAPTER 4
ARIES

Kai and I were cleaning the kitchen, but it was just more busy work to keep me distracted, while I waited impatiently for my pups to arrive. It had been a couple days longer than we'd originally expected, and I was climbing the walls.

It was funny, but when I never thought I'd see them again, I was able to go about my days and block them from the front of my mind. I never forgot them, but in order to survive, I had to teach myself to not think about them. The grief was too intense otherwise.

But, now that I knew they were on the way here, I was beside myself with excitement. I hadn't slept properly in days, and probably wouldn't even have remembered to eat, if it weren't for my pack forcing food on me every time I turned around.

"Aries, can I ask you a personal question?" I heard Kai say in a soft voice from the open fridge that he was cleaning, while I washed dishes.

"Sure, Kai. What's up?"

"Um, well, you guys all know my story about how my

own father sold me to Alpha Fremont. I just never heard your story? I was wondering, if that's okay, if you'd be willing to share it with me?"

I sighed, hating to remember my past. "It's okay, Kai. I mean, Jenny knew and Sy knows, so I can definitely tell you. I just don't really like to talk about it all that much."

"It's okay, if you don't want to talk about it. I mean, I don't want to make you remember anything painful, just because I'm nosy."

"Nah, it's not that. It's more like, I'm embarrassed, you know? But it's cool, I can tell you. Besides, I'm about to have my happy ending, as soon as that alpha cousin of Daniel's gets here with my pups, right?"

"Exactly! I'm so happy for you. I cannot even begin to imagine how hard it's been for you to be separated from them."

Straightening up, I pressed my hands to my lower back and leaned back, feeling my spine pop as I relaxed into the stretch. I stood back up, pulled off my dish gloves, and said, "This is a tea conversation. Feel like a break?"

"Sounds great, I'm at a good stopping point anyway."

"Alright, you grab the cups, I'll get the tea," I said, already moving to the stove to light a fire under my favorite kettle that I had prepped earlier for when I wanted a cup.

"Ooh, did I hear somebody say it's tea time?" Aunt Kat, the sprightly little senior citizen that we had adopted as our surrogate auntie, came walking in right as I had spoken.

Turning to smile at her over my shoulder, I said, "Hey, Auntie. I was just about to tell Kai about my embarrassing past. You're welcome to join us, if you promise not to judge me too harshly."

"Oh, honey." She spoke kindly, stopping to get a pack of cookies out of the cabinet, before going to sit at the table. "If we were all judged for our youthful indiscretions, none of us would be fit to set foot out of bed. We've all made poor choices and bad decisions, it's part of growing up. Now, get over here and tell me what yours were. If you're lucky, I might use it in a book someday!"

I laughed at the audacious little wink she shot me, and shook my head as I took the whistling kettle off the heat and filled our cups. Carrying them to the table, I bit my lip to keep from laughing as I wondered what exactly Aunt Kat wrote about in the erotic ebooks she authored. I would ask, or read one myself, but I wasn't actually brave enough to know just yet.

Placing the cups on the table, I joined Kai and Aunt Kat where they were already settled around the end of the long table. Setting my tea aside to cool a bit, I picked up a cookie and took a nibble before starting my story.

"So, Kai was mentioning that nobody really knows how I ended up with Alpha Fremont."

I took a bracing sip of tea before I continued.

"My parents died when I was a pup, and I was raised by my grandmother. It was just the two of us against the world."

"You must have been close," Aunt Kat said with an encouraging pat on my hand. "Is your grandmother still with us?"

I shook my head, biting my lip as I willed myself to stay strong. "No. She, um, she died about six months before Alpha Fremont found me. Grammy was out with friends, and they were in a car crash. She survived for about a week, but then she died in the hospital, a few months before my eighteenth birthday."

"Oh, Aries!" Kai cried out softly as he reached a hand

over to clasp mine, "You don't have to continue if it's too hard."

Shaking my head, I said: "No, I need to get this over with. If I'm going to be a dad now, I need to be able to talk about the hard things, right?"

"Oh, honey," Aunt Kat said with a sweet smile. "You've got that exactly right! The hardest thing about being an adult is being able to admit your own mistakes. If you can do that, you're a bigger man than many alphas I've known."

Blushing, I continued. "So, after Grammy died, our house had to be sold. Not only was I a kid still, but an omega at that. There just weren't any jobs that would hire me, you know?

"Anyway, the money from the house wasn't very much since there was still money owed on it, and what was left had to be used to pay off the medical bills. I was suddenly on my own, with no place to go, no food to eat, and no family to turn to. I was literally alone in the world, with just the clothes on my back."

Shuddering, I took long drink of tea, and paused for a moment to gather myself. I appreciated that Kai and Aunt Kat just sat there quietly, allowing me to have the time I needed.

"Where was I?"

"Alone on the streets," my buddy Sy said, as he came up from behind me and sat down beside me, with his baby daughter on his lap. "Sorry, I just came in

and didn't want to interrupt."

Taking a breath, I nodded. "Of course, Sy. This isn't anything that you don't already know anyway."

Looking back at the others, I went on. "At first, some of the neighbors took turns letting me sleep on their couches, but eventually people got sick of having some random kid around. And city packs aren't close like the ones here in the country are. They don't have the same pack mentality, although we do answer to an Alpha that's in charge of the territory. The Alpha tries to take care of us, but we're just too spread out, although his word is law if there's a problem."

Kai nodded knowingly at that, as I shook my head and went on. "Anyway, I soon found myself sleeping in abandoned buildings and scrounging for food. I got in with a group of other homeless kids, and they taught me how to survive by picking pockets, snatching purses, or stealing from homes when nobody was around."

I could feel my cheeks burn, as I admitted my secret shame. "I tried to pick targets that either wouldn't notice a few dollars missing, or who would be too nice to call the cops if they caught me.

"This went on for a couple months. It was the night before my eighteenth birthday, when it all went to shit." I looked up to apologize for the language, but Aunt Kat was too absorbed in my tale to care, and just gestured for me to continue.

"That night, I saw a couple of older rich ladies sitting outside eating on the patio of a little bistro. When I didn't think anyone was watching, I walked by and snatched one of their fancy purses. I probably would've gotten away with it, but there was an alpha there who saw it happen."

Kai gasped, "What did he do? He didn't hurt you, did he? Is he the one who gave you to Fremont?"

"Inadvertently, one could say," I agreed with a shrug. "But no, not directly. He chased after me, catching me about a block away. After he dragged me back to return the purse and forced me to apologize, he took me to the city Alpha and turned me in for stealing from humans."

"Oh, no, honey." Aunt Kat said sadly. "I know that you shouldn't have tried to steal it, but then again, a kid like you shouldn't have been in that position to start with, you poor lamb."

I sighed heavily, and soldiered on. "The Alpha kicked me out of his area, told me I had to leave the city and never return. He had one of his betas drive me to the outskirts of town, and I went from there on foot."

"What about the alpha that turned you in?" Kai asked me. "Did he know how bad your punishment was for a crime that wasn't even committed, when you consider that the purse was returned untouched?"

I shook my head and lifted a shoulder. "I don't know? He was young, only a year or so older than me. After he took me to the Alpha, he was sent away before I was punished. I'm sure he heard later, but I wouldn't know. I never saw him again."

"Good!" Sy snorted, "I wouldn't want to see his ass again anyway, if I were you. Screw that jerk!"

"No," I said sadly. "It wasn't his fault. He was a young, honorable alpha, you know? He didn't know my story. Besides, he was right. I shouldn't have been stealing. Maybe I should have gone to the Alpha or something? I don't know what I could have done, but I understand where he was coming from."

"But how did that lead you to Fremont?" Kai asked.

"Oh. Well, I was walking down the road, totally lost, hungry, and tired, when a car pulled up beside me. Fremont and his mate, Helga, were the ones in the car. They talked me into going with them, promising me a good life with their pack. I was stupid enough to get in the car, and the next thing I knew, I was in that cabin by the lake where he stashed his omegas."

I looked longingly at Brianne, bouncing happily on Sy's knee, thinking of my own pups. "Then when I had my first heat, Fremont forced me to mate with him, and I got pregnant with Sara. When she was born, they took her away before I even got to hold her."

Tears were streaming down everyone's faces but mine now. I was too numb to cry. Or maybe the story was too familiar? Either way, I just wanted to get it told and get back to cleaning until my pups arrived.

"When I had my next heat, it happened again, and I got pregnant with Dylan. That time, Fremont was out of town, and the doctor that Stanley called in didn't know better than to let me hold him. I got to cuddle him for about an hour before Fremont and Helga arrived to take him."

"Thankfully, I didn't catch on my next couple of heats before we were rescued. Maybe I'm broken now? I don't know or care. I have my pups, Fremont is dead, and now we will be happy here with a loving pack family. Everything that happened brought me here, and for that, I can't regret the bad parts. Even if I am embarrassed by my choices, I try not to dwell on them. Those choices gave me Sara and Dylan, right?"

"Exactly, honey," Aunt Kat said lovingly, as she got up and came over to hug me. She was so tiny, that even sitting in my chair, my head was able to rest against her shoulder. "That is exactly the right way to look at your past. The things that happened to you, the choices you made, good or bad, they all led you to where you are today, and gave you those two beautiful little ones that we will soon get to meet."

I wrapped my arms around her waist while she hugged me against her, finally at peace. It was as if by telling my story one last time, I was finally free of it. My face felt wet, and when I swiped a hand across my cheek, it surprised me to realize that I'd been crying.

I looked over to see Sy blinking his eyes and pressing a kiss to the top of Brianne's little head, while Kai silently passed me a tissue. It was good to have a family again, I thought to myself.

"Now, let's forget about being sad," Aunt Kat said a few minutes later as she sat back down in her chair. "Would you boys like to hear about a really neat toy that I discovered on one of my market research websites?"

Sy and I looked over at her curiously, while Kai desperately shook his head at us, silently imploring us to say no. *What could possibly be scary about a toy?* I wondered to myself.

"Now, I personally have never had the need for anything like this, being a beta wolf myself. But I was intrigued when I saw this, and couldn't help but think of you poor unmated omega boys when I saw this one." She cheerfully took a sip of tea, while digging her phone out of her pocket. "Hold on, let me see if I can find the link, and you can just see it for yourselves! If not, I have it on my laptop upstairs in my office."

Kai slipped down in his chair with a hand over his eyes, saying, "Fenris protect us, I'm too young to hear about these kind of things."

"Nonsense, Kai. You're mated and a father, you need to be sensible about subjects like sex. It's a perfectly natural fact of life. Besides, this one isn't for you. This is meant for unmated omegas." Aunt Kat said this in a matter-of-fact tone as she fiddled with her phone.

"Basically, it's a fantastic new vibrating dildo with a self-knotting apparatus, for when your heat strikes! If I purchased one or two, would one of you be willing to test it for me when your heat comes? It would be perfect to have someone use in a book, I think."

I looked over at Sy when I heard his sharp intake of breath, biting my lip to avoid giggling, as I saw him slip his hands over Brianne's tiny ears to protect her from hearing any more of this conversation.

"Anyway, fellows," Aunt Kat was saying, "I would so love to know if it really works, before I actually use it in a book! We could even make a blog post on my author site if you really like it enough. It would be a kindness for you to share the information with other single omegas, don't you think?"

Sy's chair scraped loudly across the floor, as he scrambled to get up and flee the room. I grinned at his pale face and shaking hands as he cuddled Brianne close, and mumbled something about needing to change the baby.

"So, Kai," I said with a smirk. "What do you think? Should I be a guinea pig for Aunt Kat and give her little toy knot thingie a try?" I busted out laughing when Kai jumped up and fled the room in Sy's wake.

Shrugging, Aunt Kat said, "I don't know why those boys are so uptight, it's not like they've never been knotted. They've had pups, right? Besides, this is just a toy. I thought it was a neat idea, and it even comes in a variety of sizes."

I laughed harder at that, and reached over and patted her hand while I made a mental note to ask my friends the next time they got on my nerves if she'd ever found the link for that dildo toy with the vibrating knot.

CHAPTER 5
MICAH

It was a long three and half days later when we finally made the turn off to the lodge. Traveling with three little ones was not something I would wish on my worst enemy, not matter how adorable the pups were. If Zane hadn't been there, I would've been completely screwed.

I realized this by the end of day one, after a day of Sara kicking the back of my seat, Dylan getting carsick three times, and baby Erin screaming bloody murder because, well, sometimes babies just needed to scream?

Angie was the wisest woman on the planet, I decided, for knowing in advance that I would need help, and then arranging for Zane to be there. I knew the guy needed a new pack too, but right now I figured I owed him a bigger fucking debt of gratitude than I could ever hope to pay.

We had to stop every couple of hours, it seemed. We had to stop and change diapers, clean puke, and then feed them so that they could puke and soil more diapers. It was a never ending cycle.

Sara was the easiest, probably because she was the

oldest and was a little more able to understand what was happening. But since she didn't wear diapers anymore, we had to include stops to take her potty. And then give her drinks that made her have to pee again. Another never ending cycle.

The part that surprised the hell out of me, though, was that I didn't mind it. It was stressful, no lie, but it was manageable with two of us there. And even though they were a lot of fucking work, the little shits were so damned adorable that I found myself enjoying it. Well, maybe except for the screaming and all of the puke. Those parts I could definitely live without.

We were about five miles from the lodge when I heard a loud thumping noise and the car began to list to one side. I shook my head silently and pulled over to the safety of the shoulder.

I was just pulling out my phone to call Daniel when a huge ass bear came loping out of the treeline. My jaw dropped as I watch it shift into a large, hairy, blonde man about my age and really fucking huge as hell.

He waved over at our car and started walking over to greet us. Stark ass naked, but then, that was kind of a thing with us shifters. Nudity wasn't anything we really noticed. Since we were all naked when we shifted, it really couldn't be helped.

"Um, Micah? Is that a bear shifter?"

"Yeah, Zane. Pretty sure that's why we just saw the man shift from a bear form. Don't you think so? I mean, maybe it's just me, but yeah. Pretty sure."

"Yeah. Whatevs, dude. *I meant,* I didn't know there really were bears! I've heard of them, but I've never seen another shifter besides us wolves. That's insane! Are you seeing how big he is?"

"Shh. Don't freak out the kids. But, yeah, he's pretty dang big."

"Mistuh Nutter Daddy?"

"Yes, Sara?" I had given up on trying to convince the girl to call me Micah. Apparently this nutter daddy shit was gonna be a thing. I could already hear Daniel now. Fucker would laugh his ass off, I knew that already.

"Dat man don' got cwoves on."

"I know, angel. He's a shifter, like we are. When he shifted back to his human form, he didn't have clothes there. Remember, how you needed me to give you clothes again after we shifted yesterday at the rest area and played in our wolf forms?"

"Otay. I member dat. Him need a nutter daddy too, huh?"

I grinned at her in the rear view mirror, "Exactly, right, angel girl. He needs someone to give him some clothes."

The dude was walking up, and I scented only friendly motives, so I told Zane and the kids to sit tight while I got out to greet him. I held my hand out, as he walked up and grasped it firmly. I was pleasantly surprised, since I'd honestly expected him to crush my hand with those huge ass mitts of his.

"Hello, there. I am Karl. I have been watching for the wolf named Micah. That is you, yes?"

He spoke so properly, with a hint of an accent. I was intrigued. Daniel had mentioned that the pack had made friends with the local bear den, and that they had scouts patrolling our woods to help protect us, since our pack was so small. Especially since our pack had so many unclaimed omegas. I just hadn't really expected to encounter one of them, at least, not so soon.

"Yeah, man. I'm Micah. I'm traveling with my buddy,

Zane, and three young pups. We were almost to the lodge, right? I think we have a flat, though."

Karl grunted and walked around to the passenger side. "Yes. There is indeed a flattened tire on this side, Micah. Do you need assistance changing it? It would be my pleasure."

I didn't see any reason to waste time posturing like an idiot alpha and turn down an offer of help, especially when I was fried from driving.

"You know what, man? That would be awesome," I said. "Let me just pop the trunk so we can get to the spare and shit."

He nodded, and just walked around to the back of the car, waiting there expectantly while I reached in through my open window and pressed the trunk release switch.

By the time I walked back to the trunk, he'd already gotten it open and was carefully setting our suitcases and belongings down on the gravel beside the car. I went to help, but he waved me back.

"No, Micah. Let me assist you. You rest, maybe see if the wee ones need anything. I was told that you have been on a long trip to bring these young wolves home to the pack?"

I stood back and rolled my head around on my shoulders from side to side, releasing the kinks. "Yeah, man. It's been a long drive, lemme tell ya."

"And you are the only driver, yes?"

"Yeah, I'm driving with an omega and the pups. Zane doesn't drive, so it's just been me. That's fine, though, you know that we alphas have to be in charge anyway, am I right? I don't know if I could ride this far with an omega driving, to be honest. Even if that does sound shitty of me to say."

Karl lifted a heavy brow sardonically, as he lifted the

tire out the trunk and leaned it against the side of the car before reaching back in for the tools.

"Ah, yes. I had forgotten you wolves' archaic distinctions between genders and classifications."

I was pretty sure that I should be pissed at that statement, but wasn't entirely sure what the put-down actually was, given how politely he spoke.

"Oh, you mean that we think that alphas are better? No, it's not like that. I mean, maybe with some wolves? For me, I just think that we each have our places in the pack, you know? Like, omegas like to tend to the house and pups, while we alphas need to protect them, and do the harder stuff."

"I believe that is what I said, is it not?"

Scratching my head, I asked, "Are things different for bears?"

"Every species is different, I suppose. But, yes, we bears know better than to think that the omega or female bears are in any way subservient to an alpha, or less able than one of us to handle mundane tasks such as driving a car. In my den, our mechanic is a female omega. Several of our hunters and patrol men are omegas."

"Seriously? But, what if they get hurt? Omegas are fragile!"

He paused in the middle of removing the old tire, and roared out a laugh. "I am sorry, Micah. It is just that the idea of an omega being fragile is laughable. Do you think that you could bear a child and give it birth? I know that is not a thing that I, myself, would want to do. Yet, omegas do it every day. No, they are the strong ones. It is us big alphas that beat our chests and roar, only to later find ourselves leaning upon their quiet strength."

"I dunno about all that, man. Although, I'll give you the

childbirth thing. No way I'm ever doing that, thanks be to Fenris, but I promise that I wouldn't want to either!" I shuddered at the thought.

Karl chuckled, as he tightened the lug-nuts on the new tire. "I take it that you are not yet mated, Micah. Do me a favor. When you find your mate, wait until six months after you've had the first child, then come find me. We will have this conversation again, and see if your ideas have not changed. I would wager you a lager that they will."

"Hah! I'll take that bet, Karl. Not that I expect to be mated anytime this decade, but sure. I doubt my views will change, though. Hey, why don't you let me buy you a lager sometime anyway? I owe you one for helping me out."

"I will remind you of this when we return to this conversation, my friend. As for a drink? I would enjoy that, indeed I would. Ask Ollie, the doctor of your pack, for my number. We will arrange to meet after you have settled in."

"Sounds great," I agreed, as I helped him load our luggage back into the trunk, after he put the flat tire in. "I'll try and catch up with you soon."

We shook hands, and Karl went back towards the woods, shifting easily back to his bear form and disappearing into the trees. I watched the gentle giant go, and then got back in the car with my make-shift little pack that were waiting.

"He seemed nice," Zane said with an amused look on his face.

I instantly knew that he'd overheard our entire conversation, so I just gave a smirk and said, "Yeah, yeah. I bet you did, what with his liberal views on how tough you omegas are."

Chuckling, Zane replied, "I admit, it was a refreshing attitude, especially from a big bear. I would have expected the exact opposite, if I'm being honest. I guess we'll have a lot discover as we get to know our bear neighbors, right?"

"Yeah, I guess we will," I agreed, pulling back out onto the road and heading for the lodge. "I just hope that I don't meet any of their hunter omegas. Especially if they're anywhere as big as he was. That might be enough to scare me off omegas for life!"

CHAPTER 6

ARIES

Kai shouted from his post by the front window, "Aries! Hurry up and get out here! The car just pulled up! They're finally here!"

I came running in from the kitchen, only to find my entire pack gathered around, waiting to meet my pups with me. Not to mention, Jenny's baby girl was arriving too. I know that Aunt Kat, Kai, and Jake were pretty excited to finally meet their missing family member. I knew for sure that Kai already counted her as part of his little brood of pups. As the father of twins, if he wanted another baby, he could definitely handle her.

Kai wrapped his arm around my waist, and we walked out the open door behind Jake and Aunt Kat, who were already headed over to the car that had just parked. Daniel was right behind me, with the rest of the pack waiting quietly inside, so as not to freak out the new guys and little ones.

My eyes were instantly drawn to the tasty view of the firm, round, muscular alpha butt that was bent into the car, but I looked away, ignoring it. I wasn't in the market for an alpha, I just wanted my babies!

When the stranger stood up and stepped away from the car, my little Dylan was sitting on his hip, and Sara was holding his hand. An omega came around from the other side with a pretty little baby on his hip, but I only had eyes for my own pups right then. I bit down on my fist, watching them with hungry eyes as the strange alpha walked up our pack's Alpha, Jake.

I wanted nothing more than to just rush over and jerk them out of his hands. I would hold them tightly to my chest, and never let them go again. But that wasn't the best way to approach this, I knew. It would be better to meet them with no pressure, to let them adjust to me and to learn with time how very much I loved them.

It would take time for us to become a family, I knew that. Time that I was more than willing to spend. My pups were worth every moment it would take to earn their trust and win their love. But I would not force it from it from them, as hard as it would be to restrain myself

When I heard the voice of the strange alpha who was greeting our Alpha, I gasped in horror. *No! It couldn't be! Fenris wouldn't be so cruel to me!* But, as I slowly pulled my eyes from my pups, and finally looked at the gorgeous alpha that held them, I saw that it was true.

The voice that I had recognized immediately did indeed match the face. It was the same alpha that had caught me stealing five years earlier and turned me in. I would have known those emerald green eyes anywhere.

Fuck. My. Life.

Ignoring my churning gut, I focused on my pups instead. They were even more beautiful in person than they had been in their picture. Thanks be to Fenris, but I saw no sign of their sire in them.

I heard Sy's voice come from over my shoulder. "Aries, my goodness. They look just like you! Look at your eyes and hair on them, they are the very picture of you! I guess that there's no doubt who's their daddy!"

Kai turned and wrapped his other arm around me as he hugged me close. "I'm so happy for you, Aries. I know that this is very hard for you, but just look at them and know that they're really here."

"Exactly," agreed Sy, as he wrapped his arms around me from my other side. "This is just the first step, dude. The important thing to remember is that now you have the chance to take all the steps and finally make them yours, like you never could before, you know?"

I nodded, too choked up to speak. Each of my omega friends held me tight, while I got myself together. With their heads resting on my shoulders, we stood there together, silently admiring my pups.

Hearing Alpha say my name, I looked up at him, and accidentally made eye contact with the alpha from my youth. He looked at me with a narrowed gaze, as though trying to place me. I knew the moment it happened, and felt my cheeks flush with shame, as his knowing eyes remembered me all at once.

Scenting the mixture of guilt, shame, anger, and remorse coming off me in waves, Kai jerked his head up and turned to look at the alpha, before looking back at me.

"What's the problem, Aries? He's Daniel's cousin, he's vouched for. What's the problem?" Kai whispered softly against my ear.

I turned and spoke in as low of a tone as I could, hoping not to be overheard while in the vicinity of other shifters with our advanced hearing. "It's *him.* He's the alpha that caught me and turned me in when I was a kid."

Both of my friends gasped and tightened their hold me, anchoring me in place, while I fought to get control of my urge to shift and run off into the woods. I agreed with my wolf that this was a good idea, but I couldn't leave my pups. Not right now, not ever again.

"Stay here with Sy, I'm going to go meet Erin. Just observe and hang back. And, for the love of Fenris, don't speak to Micah."

"Who?" I asked quizzically.

"Micah, that's his name. The alpha is named Micah," he repeated patiently when he caught my blank stare. "Now, stay here until you have control."

Kai pulled away from me, and walked over to where Aunt Kat was cooing over baby Erin, right next to Alpha, Micah, and my pups. I wondered who the omega was that was holding her, but brushed it off to focus on my own little guys. I would meet the new omega soon enough.

"Should we go closer, just enough to maybe try to let the pups learn your scent?" Sy asked me softly, ready to move at whatever pace I set.

"I don't know what to do," I replied. "It seems every option has its own set of pitfalls. Not to mention that now I have to deal with this Micah person again."

"I know, hon. It's not fair, that of all the freaking alphas on this planet, he had to be the one that's Daniel's cousin. But you'll deal with it, right? I mean, it's what we omegas do, isn't it? Deal with the shitty stuff in life?"

"You know that's right." I sighed. "Okay, Sy, let's do this thing." Reluctantly, I pulled out of my friend's hug, and reached for his hand. Grasping mine back tightly, he led me closer to where my pups were.

Daniel walked up on my other side. Putting his hand up silently, he gently squeezed the back of my neck to calm my nerves. "You seem upset, Aries. I can feel your stress. Be calm, this will be fine. Trust me."

"Are you trying to work your alpha mojo on me, Daniel?"

"Sure am, Aries. Is it working?"

"Little bit. Much as I hate to admit it."

Grinning, he dropped his hand and escorted me over to where his cousin and our Alpha were still talking.

"Alpha," Daniel interrupted them, "I thought we should introduce Aries to Micah and the pups."

Turning to me with a gentle smile, Alpha said, "Aries, come meet these guys. I know you've been waiting a long time."

Nodding hesitantly, I stepped just out of touching range, and knelt down in front of Sara. I tucked my hands in between my knees, and smiled gently as I patiently waited for her to respond. She clung to Micah's hand, her face half buried against his thick, muscular thigh.

Micah crouched down beside her, setting Dylan down on the grass, but still cradling him within the curve of his arm.

"Hi, Aries. Now that we're officially meeting, I'm Micah. I gotta admit that this is actually pretty awkward, not gonna lie. How about we just start over with each other?"

Of course he touched the elephant in the room right off the bat, mentioning our past acquaintance. *What a typical alpha jerk*, I thought. *Couldn't he have just tried to pretend not to recognize me?* Although, to be fair, it did make me respect him just a little, that he didn't try to ignore or downplay our previous connection.

"Fine, let's do that," I said through gritted teeth, willing myself to ignore the enticing scent of him. It was an intoxicating blend of bourbon and mesquite, and it was fantastic. I felt myself mentally pulling toward him, as my inner wolf paced and screamed: "*MATE, THIS IS OUR MATE!*"

I ignored that inner voice, because sometimes my wolf was a damned idiot. Instead, I focused on Sara and Dylan, eagerly soaking up the sight and scents of my pups, happy to be so close to them at last.

Micah spoke next to Sara's ear: "Angel, I want you to meet your daddy. This is Aries. He is your daddy that I told you about, and he wants so much to get to know you and love you."

Sara looked at me, her lower lip sticking out in the cutest little pout. "No, I towed you ahweady! Don' need no nutter daddy but you. You my Nutter Daddy!"

I gasped at her words, my eyes flicking towards Micah's in outraged fury. "Why is my daughter calling you 'daddy'? Are you seriously trying to steal my pups' affections now? You didn't cause enough problems for me in the past?"

He stood abruptly, lifting Dylan back up against his chest, while glaring down at me. "Amusing as it is that a scummy little snatch and grab artist like you would actually try to accuse an honorable alpha like me of being a thief, I'm sorry to say that you are wrong. I have not tried to '*steal their affections*'. Seems like when you're the first person in a pup's life to not treat them like shit, they tend to get attached. Funny how that works, isn't it? Hmm, sweet-cheeks?"

Jumping to my feet, I hissed indignantly, "How. Dare. You. Do you even know what you caused for me when you butted yourself into my life all those years ago? Do you know why my pups were even alive to be in a position for you to have to help them? No. You do not. You know jack crap, Mister. You don't know me, you don't even know the first thing about me, y-y-you cretin!"

Standing there glaring at each other, tension simmered between us that was only broken when I felt a sharp kick to my shin, followed by the fierce shout of my Sara's little voice. "Don' you tawk to my Nutter Daddy wike dat! Him good alfa! Weave us awone, you big 'toopid head!"

Dylan started whimpering then, burying his face into Micah's neck and clinging to him. Wincing as if he'd suddenly remembered the pups' presence, Micah shot me a surprisingly apologetic look and firmly said, "Sara, you may not talk to your daddy like that. I know that you don't know him yet, but we've talked about this, remember?"

He let go of her hand and brushed a hand through her curls, saying gently: "You need to be a good girl, and give your daddy a chance. And when we're having grown-up talk, you need to stay quiet and keep out of it, got me?"

Lip firmly stuck out now, she folded her little arms across her chest and glared up at me from under her silky lashes.

"Sara, I'm gonna need an answer, pup." Micah continued pushing her.

"Otay. But you my Nutter Daddy. Not dis guy."

The strange omega came closer, handing Erin to Kai with a tight smile. "Hi, I'm Zane, why don't you go ahead and take your little princess, so that I can help with the other pups."

Kai immediately reached for Erin, his face lit up like pure sunshine. Alpha looked from me to Micah, as if wondering whether he should get involved.

Daniel stepped in then, saying: "Alpha, why don't you and Kai take Erin to meet the twins with Aunt Kat? I think you guys need some family time, don't you? I'll take care of things here."

Kai, though distracted, looked at me with concern. "Do you need me, Aries? I can stay, if you need me?"

"I'm okay, Kai. Go be with your family," I replied gently. "We'll catch up later after all the pups are in bed, yes?"

"Yes, let's do that," he agreed, eagerly reaching for his mate's hand as he led him back to the lodge with Aunt Kat right behind them.

Zane turned to us then and said, "I don't want to overstep, but perhaps I could take the pups inside to go freshen up and have a snack? Sara might feel better if she's not *hangry*. The hungry-anger rage is strong with this one," he giggled. "Also, they know me now, so I don't mind helping, if that's okay?"

He looked back and forth from me to Micah, as though uncertain as to whose permission was needed at this point.

Daniel solved the momentary indecision by saying to him, "That's a perfect solution, Zane. Thank you for suggesting it. Go ahead and get these young pups inside, while the grown-ups sort this out, whatever this is, anyway."

Sara stubbornly clung to Micah's hand when Zane reached for her, while Dylan willingly went into his arms.

"No, I tay wif my Nutter Daddy. Him need me."

"It's okay, Sara, I'm just fine and so are you," Micah said gently, leaning down to kiss the apple of her chubby little cheek. He brushed her curls back, and said, "Go on now, and help Dylan, so he's not scared, okay? I'll be in to check on you soon, and your actual daddy will too. We both love you, angel. Don't worry, okay, angel?"

Sara reluctantly took Zane's hand with a final reproving look at me, and he led her inside the lodge with the other pack members. This left me alone with Daniel, Sy, and Micah now.

"Now, which one of you would like to fill me in on whatever the hell that was about?" Daniel asked us quietly.

"What's going on is that this jerk-faced cousin of yours is trying to let my pups think that he's their fucking daddy or something!" I snarled, seething with jealousy and frustration.

"Whoa, Aries. Language. Let's just calm down and talk like adults."

Sy turned to Daniel and hissed, "Seriously? There are no pups out here now, and we're all *fucking* adults here, Daniel. Or, are weak, traumatized, little omegas like us supposed to only use adorable expletives such as *gosh, darn,* or *gee-golly-willikers*? Fuck that shit. Aries has a right to be pissed off! You have no idea what the hell your cousin did to him!"

"I didn't mean to imply that omegas are weak simpletons, Sy. I would never say something like stupid that," Daniel stated calmly. "I'm just saying that we all need to be calm, and discuss whatever this is in a rational manner."

"Street thieves aren't known for their rational thought processes, cuz. Sorry to break that to you," Micah said with a derisive snort.

"So much for starting over, huh? Thanks for nothing, asshat." I yanked my shirt off and stalked toward the parking area, angrily pushing down my pants as I let my wolf take over and smoothly shifted.

I looked back at the alphas who were standing there with my dear friend, all three of them staring at me in shock, as I growled low in my throat and took off running into the trees. Fuck humanity. I needed to be a wolf for a few and just run my rage off.

CHAPTER 7
MICAH

I watched as Aries ripped the clothes furiously from his gorgeous body, willing my wolf to hold back and not follow that small, beautiful, gray and white wolf as it had run off into the trees.

I needed to not remember the sight of his lithe, naked body and ignore my lust for now. That tight little ass, though! But now was not the time to even attempt to acknowledge that he was mate. The minute that I'd caught his scent, I'd known. Even though I recognized him as the little street thief that I'd turned in several years ago, I didn't give a shit about that at all.

His spicy vanilla scent was intoxicating to me, and my wolf had screamed "*Mate! Mine!*", as soon he'd knelt down in front of Sara. It had taken every ounce of alpha strength to deny my wolf, as now was definitely not the time for that. If there *would* be a good time, based on how our interactions had gone so far.

"Micah," Daniel's voice intruded sternly. "What the hell are you going on about, calling Aries a street thief and treating him like that? He's pack, man. You want to join our pack, and this is how you greet a beloved member?"

"Because he *is* a street thief, Daniel. Remember when I was living in the city, while I was in college? And I caught a little punk trying to do a snatch and grab on some human lady's purse? That's him! I never knew what happened after I turned his ass in to our Alpha back then, but now, here he is again. And obviously, he's still a punk, but unfortunately, those pups need him. For their sake, I'll be nice and try to mend fences, is that good enough for you?"

Before Daniel could answer, the other omega that had been there with my mate stepped forward and jabbed his pointer finger into my sternum.

He fucking let me have it, screaming, "He is NOT a street punk, you alpha douche! He ended up on the Fenris-damned streets after his grandmother died. And he was only seventeen fucking years old at the time, not that you'd care! He was stealing because the city pack didn't look out for him. He was all alone, and he was just a hungry kid."

Daniel and I stared at him in shock, as he continued. "And did you hear about Alpha Fremont and how he kidnapped or bought omegas to forcibly mate them and make them whelp his pups, just so that he could try and get an alpha heir? Did you know about that part? Because that's who those pups' sire was. He was my daughter's and Erin's sire too."

Daniel reached out to touch his neck, sending out calming waves, but the guy that I'd heard him call Sy just brushed the hand away. "Don't even fucking pull your alpha mojo shit on me, Daniel. Not fucking now. I'm righteously pissed, and I don't want to calm down until I've said what needs to be said."

Turning back to me, Sy said, "That city Alpha that you

turned him in to, for that petty theft against a human? A theft that didn't even actually happen, after you prevented it? That Alpha kicked Aries out of the city. He had him dropped at the city borders, on foot, and still hungry after still not having eaten in a couple of days at that point. When a kindly seeming Alpha-pair pulled up alongside him while he was wandering down the road in an unfamiliar area, and offered him a ride, he was innocent enough to accept it, hoping for help at last."

With a pained grimace, he finished the story: "Unfortunately, that Alpha was Fremont, and you know the story from there. But do you know that when he sexually assaulted us, and I say assault, because mating is too kind of a word for what he did, his fucking mate actually stood there and watched our torment? Then, when any pups were born, they were whisked away before their carrier parent ever even had a chance to hold them. And Aries? That happened to him. Twice. TWO TIMES, Micah. That's why he doesn't know his own babies!"

He had tears running down his face as he raged at me. "That, Micah, is the price that Aries paid for trying to steal money for food. Now tell me, do you think that the petty street thief paid a high enough price, or should we punish him some more? Fuck this shit. I'm going to find my friend, and don't either of you dare to fucking follow us."

Ripping off his clothes as he muttered something under his breath about "fucking alpha asshats", he smoothly shifted into the form of a small gray wolf and took off running in the same direction that I'd seen Aries go.

"Fuck." Daniel rubbed his hands over his face and carded them back through his hair, as he paced in front of me. "I've never heard any of the omegas speak quite that graphically about what they'd been through, although obviously, Jake and I had filled in the blanks, you know? The thought of those poor young guys being put through that kind of shit, it kills me! Did you see poor Sy's face when he was telling us their story? I wish I could go back and watch Fremont die all over again. What a piece of absolute shit."

"Daniel, stop," I breathed out, dizzy with pain from hearing about what had happened to my mate. "Forget Fremont. He's dead. Tell me what I can do to make it up to Aries for being an asshole to him. I was a kid myself! I thought I was doing the right thing, and that he'd be put on probation or taken home to let his parents deal with him, you know? I never expected that he'd be kicked out of the fucking pack territory for attempted theft, you know? How do I live with what I've done to that guy? And, for the love of Fenris, how do we get those pups to accept him?"

"Chill, Micah. That's how we start, by calming down and making a plan," my cousin said, as he regained his composure and focused on my words.

I growled after a moment's thought. "I bet that city Alpha kicked him out because he knew Aries needed help and he didn't want to be bothered, so he used the incident as an excuse to get rid of him. What a piece of shit, you know?"

Daniel nodded. "Okay, Micah. I think your first step is to go in and hang out with the pups. They're obviously attached to you, *Nutter Daddy*."

"Fuck you, Daniel."

The bastard just grinned at me, and continued. "Talk to them, pave the way for Aries. Then, when they're in bed tonight, talk to him and apologize. You didn't know the whole story back then, and you damned sure never would have wanted things to go the way they did for him, I know you better than that."

"There's one other problem, Daniel."

"What's that?"

"He's my mate. My wolf recognized it the moment I scented him earlier."

"Well, shit. That puts a whole other spin on it then, doesn't it?"

"Any advice?"

"From me? I'm the last person you want to ask for advice about claiming your mate, since I don't have one yet. Or even know if I ever will, for that matter. If you want advice, I'd talk to Jake and Kai. Together. Kai is close to Aries, and he'd be willing to help you, once he knows that you're not going to hurt his friend."

"Yeah, that's a hard no. I'm not gonna ask the Alpha-pair that I just met for mating advice. Next idea?"

"Back to what I said before then. Help him connect to his kids, apologize, grovel if necessary. Give it time, and it will probably work out on its own."

"Really? That's your sage advice? Give it time? Use the pups? Kiss ass?"

"Hey, I told you I was the last person you wanted mating advice from."

I grinned, clapping a hand on his shoulder as we slowly walked towards the lodge. "Yeah, I think you're right about that, cuz. That's okay. I'll figure it out, eventually. I hope so, anyway. Either way, I do owe the guy an apology. I thought I did the right thing back then, but my actions sure as hell fucked his life up. I'm not sure if I know how to even begin to make that up to him, but I'll try like hell, if he will let me."

CHAPTER 8

ARIES

I felt much better after my run in the woods. It had centered me, to be in my wolf form, running carefree without the burden of human concerns. I was on the trail of a plump rabbit when Sy encountered me. He joined me on my hunt, and we worked together to catch it.

We played with it for a bit, probably scaring a few years off the poor thing, before finally letting it hop away. I'm a catch and release type of hunter, because I honestly don't care for the idea of eating raw meat, even if my wolf disagrees.

After we tired ourselves out, we went and stretched out in the sun on the bank of the creek that runs through our woods. It was a good day to be in wolf form, especially with my friend there.

When Sy shifted to his human form, I knew he wanted to talk. I chuffed at him, but shifted back nevertheless. We sat there quietly for awhile, lounging in the soft grass, with the sun filtering down on us through the trees.

"Aries, don't kill me."

"Fuck, Sy. You told him, didn't you?"

"Yeah, he needed to know what happened after he turned you in. I'm sorry if that betrayed your trust, but he needed to know if you guys are gonna ever have a chance to patch things up and be pack, you know?"

"There's another problem though, Sy."

"What's that?"

"He's my mate. I caught his scent earlier the moment I got close to him."

"What the fuck? No wonder you were so pissed off." Sy rolled over and sat up, staring at me for a long time before he started laughing.

"I know, I know. Of all the damned, stupid alpha-holes, right?"

"Fenris must have a seriously warped sense of humor, to make him your fated mate."

"Hey, now. He's not that bad! And honestly, he turned me in back then because he was a young alpha, full of honor, you know? Everything is black and white at that age. If it happened now, he would probably at least ask me a few questions, I think."

"Wow, you have it bad already, if you're sticking up for him."

"Well, he did rescue my pups, and then spend a week caring for them. That's kind of a big deal, and I can't ignore that. Plus, he's Daniel's cousin, and they're pretty close, I think. That right there means that he's probably a good guy. I'm just jealous of how close he is to my pups. And pissed that he's, well, him. If that makes sense."

"Yeah, I get it. And Daniel's a pretty good guy, even if he is a little stiff. Micah seems a little cooler than him, although he is still a fucking alpha-douche. But he does get mad props for taking care of your pups. And he was obviously good to them, or they wouldn't be so close to him. It's a tough one, A."

"What is it with you and alphas, anyway? You avoid them like the plague, even Seth, and didn't you used to be besties with him and his brother? Seth's always been super sweet and respectful of us, so I don't get your deal with him."

"I don't want to talk about Seth. Let's focus on you, for now. We'll deal with my shit another day."

"Okay," I sighed. "But a good friend would have let me change the subject, when I tried to just there."

"And a good friend wouldn't change the subject from one alpha-hole to a bigger alpha-hole."

"Touche," I giggled. "Should we go back soon?"

"Yeah, Brianne's gotta be up from her nap now, and we both know that you aren't going to build a relationship with your own little ones by sitting here with me."

I threw a handful of grass at him, and shifted back to my wolf form. Sy shifted back too, and after we both took a refreshing drink of water from the creek, we ran back to the lodge. It was time to man up, deal with my mate, and get to my kids.

When we got back, the pack was just sitting down to dinner. A kids' area had been set up in the corner, across from our big dining table. My pups were sitting there on the benches of an adorable little picnic style table. Brianne, Erin, and the Alpha's twins, Jules and Jenna, were all lined up behind them in a row of high chairs.

It was the cutest shit that I'd ever seen in my life. Also, it totally made me realize how overrun our pack was with pups now! Six little ones, and four of them were under a year old? Damn. If we weren't careful, the pups were going to outnumber the adults pretty soon.

"Aren't they just the cutest?" Kai greeted us as we came in the door.

"Wow, I was just thinking that we better watch out or the pups will soon outnumber the adults around here!"

"Funny, that's exactly what I said when I came in," Micah said quietly from a seat at the back of the table.

I nodded at him politely, but didn't respond. I was willing to try and fix things with him eventually, but first I wanted to focus on my pups. They needed to come first right now.

"Okay, everyone sit. The pups are handled, and if they need anything, Ryan and Luke have agreed to help out with them. I want all the adults to relax tonight. We need it, some of us more than others," Alpha said as he pointedly looked from me to Micah. I nodded my agreement, and took a seat next to Sy.

We both kept our heads down and ate our meal, as the conversation flowed around us. Kai was gushing about Erin to anyone who would listen. I smiled, thinking about how different that pup's life would be now, as the niece and now daughter of the Alpha-pair. Her mom, Jenny, would've been so happy to know that the little one was finally here with her family.

Thinking of my own pups, I looked up at Micah, only to see him watching me. Biting my lip to avoid saying anything snarky, I asked him about Dylan instead.

"So, um, Micah. I noticed that Dylan didn't talk before. Is he just shy?"

My heart melted at the way his eyes lit up at the

mention of my son. Truly he couldn't be all bad, if he loved my pups this much, right?

"Good question, Aries. I wish I knew. I haven't heard a word from him since I found him. I don't know if he can talk or if Sara just does all the talking for him, and he can't get a word in, you know?"

Grinning at the thought of my stubborn daughter, I said, "We should maybe look into that then. Although, he is just two, so that could be a factor? I don't know."

"If I may intrude," Doctor Ollie, our pack doctor and resident bear, cut in. "I have seen things like this before. I would like to examine him before you worry about any other problems. There are many physical issues that can cause a child to be non-verbal."

"Shouldn't he be talking by now though, Doc? Do I need to worry?" I asked him hesitantly. "Maybe he's just a late bloomer?"

"That could be," Doc replied, "but like I said, a physical examination is your first step. I would also like to examine the girl. She has speech problems that may also have an underlying physical cause."

Micah bristled at that, before I even had a chance to get upset. He leaned toward Doc Ollie and said in a low snarl, "Are you trying to say that there's something wrong with that little angel? Because that pup is perfect, and I won't let anyone talk shit about her!"

Everyone at the table went silent, watching the exchange. Doc Ollie just took a sip of his soup before he calmly responded.

"I didn't mean to upset you, young man. I was merely suggesting to the pup's parent that she may have a physical reason for her unintelligible speech patterns."

"Unintelligible? What the actual fuck? Are you saying my girl is stupid?"

"Excuse me," I butted in, "but she is *my girl*, and Doc said no such thing! He simply meant that nobody can understand her."

"I understand her just fine. Maybe everyone else needs to clean the wax out of their ears, or else just not talk to her if they have a problem. There's nothing wrong with my angel."

Glaring at him, I said through clenched teeth, "You mean, *my girl*, and *my angel*. She is nothing to you, and if she needs medical help, I will get it for *my pup*. You need to step off and remember that I am her parent."

Doc Ollie was blushing furiously as he said, "Please, please. I did not mean to offend, I was simply suggesting—"

"It's okay, Doc," I interrupted him with an apologetic smile. "I am her parent, and I understand your concern. I will bring her by tomorrow if you have time. If there's an issue, we need to know now while she's still young enough to fix it, right?"

Micah banged the flat of his hand down on the table, the noise startling in the quiet room. "Damn it, Aries! Can you wait until you've known the kid at least five minutes before you start trying to fix imaginary problems? And don't fucking tell me who is or isn't my angel. I love that girl and she loves me, so you're just gonna have to deal with that shit, because it ain't changing."

I stood, pushing my chair back, and leaned over the table with both hands resting on its surface, as I snarled across at Micah: "You will not tell me how to parent, Mister I've-known-the-pup-for-a-week-and-think-I-know-best!"

Micah stood, mirroring my position as he growled right

back at me: "And you won't tell me how I feel either, Mister I've-been-a-dad-for-five-minutes-and-suddenly-I'm-a-fucking-expert!"

"Enough!" Alpha spoke firmly, his power swirling in the air. "You two take it outside or table it for now. The pack is trying to enjoy a meal, not deal with your beef. Now either sit down and eat, or go fight somewhere else. This ends now."

"Sorry, Alpha," I muttered. "I'm not hungry anyway now. I'm going to go see if everything is set up in the pups' room for the night. Excuse me, everyone."

I walked out of the room, and ran upstairs to the pups' new room that was right next door to my own on the second floor. The connecting rooms had been given to me when we found out about my pups. Until today, I had lived in the dormitory on the third floor with the other unmated members of the pack.

The second floor was where the family rooms were, along with the rooms for weaker or younger members of the pack. Aunt Kat, the young omega teens Luke and Ryan, and of course, Sy and Brianne all lived up here.

The Alpha family also had their suite of rooms of here too. Doc Ollie stayed here in a room on this floor as well, when he wasn't staying in his own cabin at the end of the row of cabins that sat in a long row next to the large lodge.

Aunt Kat's writing office, and a large playroom/nursery/daycare set-up where the pups were kept during the day, while their parents were busy working around the lodge, were also on this floor. The omega members of the pack worked in teams to man the nursery, with the occasional help from alphas who were good with kids.

I smoothed a hand over the already perfectly spread bed that Sara would have now, before walking over to check on

Dylan's. Both twin sized beds were pushed up against the wall on opposite sides of the room, with toddler bed rails in place on the side that was open to the room.

I didn't really know if they were necessary, but it made me feel safer to know that my pups wouldn't fall out of bed during the night. I was leaned over plumping Dylan's pillow, when I smelled Micah's delicious scent and felt his eyes burning into my ass.

I stood up and spun around to find him leaning against the frame of the open door in a deceptively casual stance. His hands were tucked into his pants pockets, and he had a sheepish smile on his face.

"Sorry again, Aries. I guess I'm not that good at keeping the peace when it comes to you, am I?"

"It's just, whatever." I waved a hand as if to shoo him away. "I'm fine. We should just avoid each other or something, that will probably work for the best."

"Either that, or we could pretend we're fucking adults and just actually fix our shit? I mean, it is an option, right? Or, are you not up to adulting right now?"

I bit into my bottom lip and prayed to Fenris for patience. "Just because I don't want to talk to you, doesn't mean that I'm not a fucking adult, Micah."

"Never meant to imply that you're not an adult," he said, as his eyes roamed my body wantonly. "You're definitely all man, from what I can see. I'm just saying that maybe you don't feel like acting like one when it comes to me."

I stalked over and got right up in his space, until we were nearly chest to chest. Although, given his foot or so of height advantage, it was more accurately my face to his chest. His finely chiseled muscular chest...

Glaring up into his amused face, I said, "Just because I

think you're an asshat doesn't mean that I'm not acting like an adult. It means that I can spot an alpha-douche when I see one."

"Alpha-douche, huh? Classy, babe," he said with a smirk.

"Don't call me fucking babe." I growled.

"Babe."

"Douche."

Before another word was spoken, the fucker leaned down and kissed me! He lips pressed firmly against mine, and when I gasped in shocked arousal, he slipped his tongue right through the opening my lips made.

Before I knew what was happening, I was spun around and pressed up against the wall under his larger body, while he kissed me. The world ceased to exist in that moment, all I knew was the feel of his tongue wrestling with mine.

He had one hand wrapped around the back of my neck, holding me in place, while his other hand snaked out to hold my hand that wasn't resting on his chest. How my hand got onto his firm chest, I couldn't tell you.

I only became aware of all this, as well as the hard erection that was now pushing against my gut where his hips were pushed up against me, when I felt something cold and metallic encircle my wrist and heard the snick of a locking mechanism snap into place.

"What the fuck?" Micah pulled his lips away from our kiss and looked down at our hands, which were now handcuffed together.

I peeked my head around his large arm to see Aunt Kat and Kai standing there behind him. Aunt Kat had a knowing smirk on her aged face, while my poor friend just looked ashamed and afraid.

"Watch your language, young man. You may be big, but I can still take a whip to a young alpha ass like yours if need be. Although, it would be a shame to mark up something that fine." Aunt Kat glanced at me and added, "Unless you're into that sort of thing?"

My eyes widened, as my jaw dropped open.

"Good." She nodded and said, "You two looked like you were finally going to do something about fixing the problems between you, and I think that it will help you if neither of you can run off."

"Give me the key, Aunt Kat. I need to get my pups bathed and put to bed, I can't be handcuffed to an alpha while I'm doing that."

Micah seemed incapable of speech at this point; his head just whipped back and forth between me and Aunt Kat as we talked.

"No, you don't. All you need to do tonight is get things fixed with your alpha here. And don't try to lie to me, even a beta like me can smell the pheromones sparking off you two. It would be sweet if you weren't both so damned stubborn!"

"Aunt Kat, I appreciate your concern, but my pups—"

"Will be just fine," she finished for me. "I've talked to young Zane, and he will see them to bed tonight. I know it hurts, boy, but those pups are familiar with him right now anyway. You need to stick with your plan and let the relationship happen naturally. They've had a long day, and their daddy needs to deal with his own shit anyway."

"Aunt Kat, unlock these men," Alpha said as he walked into the room and saw what was going on. He reached out to take the key from her, but she stepped away and shook her head

"No, and nobody else is getting the key to separate them

either! Like I said, they need to fix their shit. The only way that's ever going to happen is if somebody pushes the issue, and that's what I'm doing." With that, she took the key in her hand and stuffed it down into her bra, where none of us would ever dream of reaching. Ugh, even the thought was both embarrassing and gross.

Micah grinned suddenly, chuckling in amusement at Aunt Kat. "You know what? You're right. And, you said the pups will be taken care of?"

"I give my word," Aunt Kat declared imperiously.

"Okay, then if there's somewhere a bit more private we can go, I think that my mate and I have some unsettled business that needs to be discussed."

"Your what?" Kai gasped out, as the Alpha smirked and reached into his pocket for a key ring.

Taking a single key off, he handed it to Micah, saying, "Good for you, man. Congratulations to you both. Second cabin, to the left of the lodge, I'm sure you saw them earlier. We'll all watch over the pups, you guys take as long as you need. I don't want to see or hear from either of you until you've either claimed or killed each other, okay?"

"Excuse me," I interrupted, "but I don't appreciate this, and I need to see to my pups more than I need a mate right now!"

Kai and Aunt Kat both smiled kindly at me as they shook their heads. But Alpha answered and said gently, "No, Aries. The pups need a parent who is calm and not ready to kill the alpha that they both already love. If you're fated, you won't be at rest until you accept it."

Aunt Kat walked over to stand next to Alpha and said, "Take this time, young man. Go work on things with your fine young alpha here. I know you want to be with your pups, but right now you need to put Micah first. Once you guys figure things out, maybe you'll be able to actually work together, and the pups will be better for it. Trust an old lady on this one."

Before I had a chance to argue further, Micah scooped me up with his free arm, and hoisted me over his shoulder and carried me out of the room. Before I could scream bloody murder or kick him with my knee like I planned, I heard Sara's little voice.

"Wot you doin', Nutter Daddy?"

"Hey, angel! I need you to stay with Zane and your brother, and be a good pup for everyone, okay? I have to go somewhere with your daddy right now."

"Otay. You be back toon?"

"I'll be back as soon as I'm done with your daddy here. We have some grown-up stuff to do, okay? When we get back, we will come and see you the very first thing, that sound alright?"

"Otay, but if da daddy guy don' be nice, you 'pank him, otay?

"Okay, angel, I'll spank him if I think he needs it. Watch this." Micah landed a smack on my ass that made me yelp and I heard Sara giggle. Wriggling on his shoulder, I reached my free hand around to the soft flesh at his waist and gave it a pinch, which only landed me another swat on my ass. Fucking alphas.

Zane muttered something about the pups' bath time and thankfully got them moving again, while Micah called back to them, "Good night, pups. I love you! Remember to be good for Zane!"

"Otay, Nutter Daddy!" I could see Sara's little face now as they walked past us, and she looked up at me with a highly amused grin. Dylan was cuddled up against Zane's shoulder. I rolled my eyes and smiled down at her, hoping that maybe things would work out, and she would accept me someday soon as her father. Her and Dylan both. The fact that she'd referred to me as that daddy guy gave me hope that this was indeed a possibility.

CHAPTER 9

MICAH

I carted my mate's tight little body downstairs, past the knowing smirks of the other alphas and the wide-eyed faces of the pack omegas. We went right out the door, and I easily jogged over to the second cabin.

Once I got the door unlocked, and locked it behind me, I set the key on a little table by the door.

"You hungry?" I grunted, unsure what else to say right now.

"Oh, now you want to talk to me? I didn't know cavemen were capable of speech like us mere mortals."

"Shut up, Aries. If you weren't so damned pig-headed, we wouldn't be in this mess. Now, it's a simple question. Are. You. Hungry."

"No. I just want to go to sleep, pretend everything is hunky-dory, and maybe Aunt Kat will unlock us in the morning."

"Yeah, um, I don't think it's gonna be that easy," I said as I found the bedroom and carefully deposited him on the bed, while I tried not to pull on the cuff that bound us together. I sat down next to him, ready to deal with his temper that I felt sure was about to erupt. At least now I knew where Sara got her little feisty streak from.

"Why not? I can act like an adult, if you can. As long as we're not fighting, I don't see why Aunt Kat wouldn't unlock this cuff."

"Because that's not her intention. She wants us to sort out the tension between us. It will be readily obvious if we haven't when we go back there in the morning."

With a sigh, Aries flopped back and stretched out on the surprisingly firm mattress. "I don't know what you think we're supposed to do to solve things. It's not like we can go back in time and I can suddenly not have tried to take that woman's purse. Honestly? I'd probably still have tried, even if I had known you were there watching. I was that hungry. I hadn't eaten in a couple days, and I was just desperate at that point."

Laying back beside him, I looked at the white ceiling as I carefully chose my words. "I'm guessing that Sy told you what he shared with me?"

"Yeah. Can we not go into all that? I don't want to talk about Fremont, or any of that shit. It's over, he's dead, I have a safe home in a new pack that accepts me, and my pups have been found and returned to me. The end."

"Not the end, Aries. What about us?"

"There is no us."

"But there should be. I know that you feel this pull as strongly as I do, it would be impossible not to. Not to mention that I could feel it in our kiss."

"I can't do this. I'm not sure if I even want a mate, to be honest. It would be nice, and my pups love the hell out of you, but I'm pretty broken, Micah. I'm not the sweet little omega that a traditional alpha like you would want."

I turned to look at him. "What makes you think I'm a

traditional alpha? I admit that I can be heavy-handed at times, but I'm flexible, and young enough to learn how to be more open minded. Don't pigeonhole me, Aries. You don't know me well enough. Yet. And I'll give you the same courtesy."

He looked back at me with mild surprise, but nodded before turning his head away. "Even if we could be compatible, would you honestly want a used up omega like me? You could have anyone, Micah. I'm not good enough for you."

Turning on my side, I used my free hand to grasp his chin and turn his face back towards mine. The tears in his eyes melted me, as I said huskily, "Aries. Don't ever say that you're not good enough. You are one of the strongest people I've ever met. When Sy told me your story? Damn. I can't imagine what you've been through. But it was not your fault. You didn't ask to be assaulted and forced into whelping pups for some narcissistic lunatic."

"Maybe not," he whispered, closing his beautiful, chocolate colored eyes. "But I did get into that car in the first place. Even a grade school kid knows better than to get into a stranger's car."

"You were hungry, desperate, and all alone, sweetheart. You just trusted the wrong people. They're the ones who were at fault in that scenario, not you. Never you."

"What if you want pups of your own someday? I never caught again, after Dylan. Maybe I'm broken now."

"And maybe Fenris took pity on you and didn't give you another babe to be stolen from your arms, hmm? And even if we never have a pup together, you'd already be giving me two to love. I adore your pups, Aries, that doesn't change whether we get together or not. Those little shits weaseled their way into my heart from the get-go. I'm pretty sure that Sara is serious about keeping me, anyway.

You should probably just try to accept that at some point," I teased.

Blinking his tears away, Aries smiled shyly at me. "I just think you could do better, Micah. I mean, think about it."

I wiped away his tears with the pad of my thumb and leaned in to gently kiss his cheek, before saying, "I can't do better than a fated mate, Aries. Nobody can. Fenris made you just for me, and me for you. Your past is what made you into the person that you are, and that person is beautiful. If you don't accept my claim, you know that I'll never find another who would complete me, it's not possible. That's the whole thing works with fated mates, you know?"

He looked at me for a long moment, before he sighed and said, "I know. And I won't either. I just didn't expect to ever find my fated mate, and then here you are, and you're you, and I just..."

"Just what, sweetheart?"

"I just don't know how to do this. What if I'm not enough for you?"

"Spin that around, babe. What if *I'm* not enough for *you*? But we both know that Fenris wouldn't have designed us for each other if we didn't already complete each other in every way. This is just our human sides fighting what our wolves already know."

Aries smiled shyly, before leaning over to cautiously press his soft lips to mine. Threading my fingers through his on the hand that was cuffed to mine, I rolled closer to him and deepened the kiss.

He parted his lips, tentatively thrusting his tongue toward mine, while I held myself back and let him explore. Braver now, he rubbed his tongue around mine, licking along the inside of my mouth while running his free hand up to grab onto my arm. Pulling himself closer to me, I felt his stiff cock push up against my hip as he lost himself in our kiss.

With a groan, I rolled completely on top of him, grinding my own erection against his through our jeans. The friction was almost enough to make me lose my nut like a damned teenager. Soon, we were grappling with each in a fury of hands, lips, and tongues, and I knew that naked time needed to start happening real damned fast.

Aries' hand ran up under my shirt and brushed across my nipple, making me gasp with tortured pleasure.

"Oh, you like that, huh?" My little mate broke away from our kiss and was nuzzling my alpha scent gland, where his claiming bite would go later.

"You have no idea, babe. I'm just trying to figure out how to get these shirts off with our hands cuffed together."

He pulled his head back and smirked at me. "Who says our shirts are coming off, alpha?"

"This does," I replied, reaching down to cup his rock hard cock.

Biting his lip, a quirk of his that was fast becoming a favorite of mine, he said, "Does that mean that, umm. I mean, are we going to..."

"Are we going to claim each other?"

He nodded silently, his velvety chocolate eyes gazing at me hesitantly.

"Do you want to? I don't want to push you, sweetheart."

"No. I mean, yes." He rolled his eyes in frustration, as he tried to explain. "I meant, no you're not pushing me, but yes, I think I do want that."

"You think? Because there's no going back if we do it, sweet-cheeks. You know that as well as I do."

He nodded shyly. "I meant, I want to if you're sure you want me."

"Baby, I could never not want you. I can't wait to make you mine, so if you're sure, then this is happening."

"I'm sure."

That's all it took. I reached down and solved the shirt problem by ripping his shirt right off his body, only pausing for a moment to take in his gorgeous, tanned skin and flat brown nipples, before ripping my own off as well.

We both frantically started unfastening our jeans and kicking off our shoes as we pushed, pulled, and yanked the offending articles of clothing off our bodies until we were both fully naked in each other's arms.

Aries stilled for moment, gazing up at me from under his thick lashes, as I settled over him. Brushing the back of my hand along the curve of his jaw, I smiled down gently at him, amazed that Fenris had gifted me with such a gorgeous mate.

Clasping our handcuffed hands together, I moved our arms out to the side, as I sat up and knelt between his thighs. My eyes roamed hungrily over his body, taking in each dip and swell of his lithe yet muscular form. I leaned over and kissed him softly, before running my tongue down his neck. Nuzzling his omega gland, I inhaled that intoxicating sweet scent of spiced vanilla again, before moving down to explore his body with my mouth.

I nipped at the small, dark brown nipple on his solid chest, then kissed the pain away, as he writhed and moaned from the attention. I licked a line across his pecs, and stopped to tease his other nipple into attention. Continuing my tongue's journey across his flesh, I stopped briefly to breathe in the pure scent of masculine musk as I buried my face into his armpit, before licking down his ribs and across his abdomen.

Pausing long enough to flick my tongue into his cute

little navel, I followed the faint pleasure trail that led down from there to his manhood. Ignoring the obvious, I licked along the crease between his hip and thigh, and nipped my way down his inner thigh.

"Micah! Quit with the teasing," Aries whimpered. "I need you."

I could smell his need, the scent of our joint arousal filling the room. I looked at the slick juice seeping from his omega hole, and pushed his legs further open, so that I could get in there to get a taste of him.

"Fuuuck," he groaned, as I licked his hole with the flat of my tongue, lapping up his sweet juices. Aries moved his free hand down to grab his twitching cock, as I licked up across his taint and suckled his balls into my mouth. Reaching over, I batted his hand away, before releasing the tight sac and finally running my tongue up his cock from root to tip.

He was packing an average sized cock; it was the perfect girth to wrap my hand around, but not too long to suck all the way in to the back of my throat. I bobbed my head up and down it a few times, sucking my cheeks in while I watched the reactive expressions that flitted across his expressive features.

I lapped the precum that was dripping from his slit, savoring his taste before I swirled my tongue around that fat, mushroom-shaped head and down along the prominent vein running down the underside of his shaft.

Not ready for him to come just yet, I ignored his whimpering moans and licked my way back down to that sweet omega hole, needing another taste of that nectar seeping from it. I licked his hole clean, teasing my way around the tight rim of muscle, relaxing it open with my tongue.

Aries' hips jerked when I speared my tongue inside his

tight hole, my face buried between the firm, round cheeks of his hairless ass as I fed there. He lifted his knees up to his chest, opening up to give me better access as he ground against my face and groaned his delight.

The juicy slick was seriously flowing from his hole now, and I lapped it up as fast as I could, not wanting to waste a drop of my mate's essence. Putting my free hand up to grab his cock, I gripped it firmly and tugged on it a few times to push him over the edge.

His abdominal muscles contracted as his head and shoulders lifted from the bed, eyes squeezed tightly shut in a face contorted by the overwhelming pleasure I was causing.

"Nnnnnggggghhhhh," he grunted, as a thick rope of cum shot out over my hand and across his torso. I left his ass, and moved up to lick it away, eagerly lapping up every drop until his body was clean, though wet from my tongue.

While he was still riding the high of orgasm, I lined my big alpha cock up with his hole and leaned over him to ask, "Are you ready for me to fill you now, babe? To make you mine?"

"Please, alpha. Make me yours," he panted, still hungry for more.

That was all I needed to hear, and with one smooth thrust, I pushed through his loosened rim and glided smoothly inside, until I was fully seated with my heavy balls pushed up against his ass. I stilled for a moment, ignoring my urge to fuck until I knew that he was ready for me to move.

"Wrap your legs around my waist," I grunted, at his nod of encouragement.

He did, and I put my free hand under his back, lifting him up so that we were chest to chest with him sitting on my lap, as I knelt there on the bed with my cock embedded in his ass. I bent his arm back behind him, the one that was handcuffed to mine. With my free hand, I gripped his hip and slowly began to thrust in and and out.

I started slowly, increasing the speed and pressure of my thrusts until I was pounding in and out of him, fucking up into him as his legs squeezed around my waist. He gripped my neck with a firm grasp of his free hand for leverage, while he leaned back and rode my cock with wild abandon.

"Fuck, babe, I'm not going to last for long. I can already feel the knot forming, ahh, fuuuuck," I moaned as my knot expanded for the first time ever. Thickening quickly, it filled his hole as I frantically humped that tight ass, until my knot finally grew so big that I was unable to pull it out again.

Aries writhed up against me, rubbing his cock off against my abs, where we were now tightly clenched together. My knot rubbed against that bundle of nerves inside his ass that gave the most pleasure, and I watched as his dazed eyes rolled back and he groaned aloud. His ass tightened around me, and he began to come at the same time as I began releasing my load into him.

"Now, omega. Claim me," I growled. Lining my teeth up over his scent gland, I bit down at the same time that his teeth broke the flesh over my own alpha gland.

Time stood still for a moment, as our souls merged and our spirits joined together. I could feel his pleasure as he rode my cock, and through the same bond, I knew he could feel what I felt with his tight ass squeezing around my knot. Once I was back in my own head, I licked his shoulder clean where it had bled from my bite, while he did the same to mine.

Turning my face for a kiss, his lips were right there searching already for mine. Legs cramping, I eased our sweaty bodies back down onto the bed. Not wanting to crush him with my heavier weight, I rolled us over until he was on top of me. We would be locked together for Fenris only knew long, until my knot went down again.

Aries shuffled and shifted until he was resting over me in a tight, little ball, his legs drawn up across my hips where he straddled me. Every time my mate shifted, it would tug on my knot a little. Not enough to hurt, but enough to make me automatically thrust again, my greedy cock searching for more pleasure even though we were both exhausted.

We passed out at some point, after we both came again more than once from the crazy amount of stimulation we were both getting through my swollen knot. Our bodies were sticky with cum and sweat by the time we slept. I woke up at some point a few hours later, to find myself being ridden again by my mate.

His entire body was flushed, hot to the touch, and pouring sweat, as he frantically writhed and wiggled on my hard cock. It took a moment for the fog of sleep to clear, when I suddenly realized that our claiming must have brought on his heat. That was the last coherent thought I had before I spent the next few hours fucking and being fucked by my desperate mate's needy hole.

The next morning, I woke up to find Aries watching me with a soft smile and a shy blush on his cheeks, as he sat there straddling my hips.

"What's the matter, babe?" I asked sleepily, before I yawned and tried to stretch my stiff back. "You okay? You have a weird look on your face."

"I'm okay. I just, well, I kinda feel like I may have taken advantage of you during the night."

Snorting out a laugh, I reached up with my free hand to cup his face. "Trust me, sweet-cheeks. The pleasure was all mine. Well, maybe both of ours? But, yeah, I definitely got my share. No need to ever worry about wearing out my cock. That's every alpha's fantasy, right there. Besides, you can't help it if you woke up in heat, you know?"

"Yeah, but that's never happened like that before. And my heat wasn't even due for another month or so."

"I've heard that meeting your mate can bring it on early, maybe that's what happened? Because we claimed each other?"

He nodded, his eyes looking thoughtfully off to the side as he considered what I'd said. "Well, anyway. I wish we could take a shower, and find some food, but that will be difficult with these cuffs still on." With an adorable blush, he continued, "Plus, I kinda really need to pee."

"You know that there's an obvious solution that one of us really should have considered last night, right?"

"What's that?" he asked curiously.

"We shift. If we go to wolf form, the cuffs will be too large and just fall right off for us."

His jaw dropped as he gaped at me. "And you couldn't have maybe thought of that before we ruined our shirts?"

"Baby." I grinned back at him. "If we'd shifted with our clothes on, they all would have been ripped to shreds. At least this way, we still have our pants, right?"

"True," he agreed and slipped off me, smoothly transitioning into his gorgeous little gray and white wolf. He stepped out of the cuff as I quickly shifted too, letting the cuff fall off my own arm.

Our wolves sniffed each other appreciatively for a few

minutes, before Aries shifted back and headed to the bathroom. I shifted back too, waiting for the toilet to flush before I followed him into the bathroom when I heard the shower start.

I took a piss, and then paused in front of the mirror while I admired the new claim mark on my neck before I joined my mate in the shower. I didn't know how long we had until his heat hit him again, so I contented myself with just getting us clean rather than trying to get up to any naughtiness in the shower. That could wait for another day. Right now, I wanted to see about getting my mate some food after we were cleaned up.

We had just gotten our pants on after our shower when I heard a knock at the cabin door. I went to answer it, while Aries went to get a drink of water.

"Hey, cuz. Looks like you two figured things out," Daniel drawled with a smirk, eyeing the mating mark on my neck. Sy was with him, carrying a basket that smelled delicious.

"We've got company bearing what smells like food, should I let them in?" I called out to Aries, while grinning broadly back at my cousin with smug pride.

"Oh, shut up," Sy said, pushing past me, and shoving the heavy basket into my hands as he went by. Daniel shrugged and followed him as I stepped back, opening the door wider.

"Ooh, you really did bring food!" Aries squealed, making a beeline for the basket.

I held it up over my head, grabbing his hand instead and pulling him toward the little round table that sat in the alcove across from the tiny kitchen in this main room of the cabin.

"I know your ass isn't planning to leave any time soon, so you might as well join us," I said to Daniel, as I watched Sy stroll over ahead of us and take a seat at the table. Releasing my mate's hand, I let him pick a seat, before I took my own right beside him. My cousin flipped the remaining one around, and straddled it with his arms resting on the back.

"How did you know that we would need food?" Aries asked Sy, when I opened the basket and began pulling out fruit and muffins. I saw sandwiches and other yummy items like nuts and cookies, but I left them there for now and set the basket down on the floor by my feet.

Sy rolled his eyes. "Please. With the pheromones you two were throwing off when you left last night? We figured you'd either be mated or dead. It was a fifty-fifty thing, but just in case, I thought I should probably bring food."

Aries grinned at his friend while he munched contentedly on a chocolate muffin. "How are my pups today? Did they do okay with their first night in the new place?"

"They were just fine, dude. Don't sweat it. From the way things smell in here," Daniel said, pausing as he sniffed the air that was redolent with the smell of omega heat, "I think you should just trust us to mind them for a few days. They can adjust to the pack while you two, er, adjust to each other."

I smirked knowingly as I watched Aries raise a brow at my cousin. "You seriously expect me to just, what? Stay locked away with Micah and fuck his brains out for days on end while my pups form new attachments with the rest of pack instead of getting to know their own father?" He spoke mildly, but I could feel his very real feelings of outrage through our bond.

Reaching out a hand, I cupped his neck to calm him down, while Sy spoke up. "Aries, we all know how much you've longed for those pups, and how very dear they are to you. But you are obviously in heat, and that is not something that I think you really want your pups to see, am I right?"

My mate looked down at the table as he blushed, but quickly nodded in agreement to that quite apt statement.

Sy continued: "Then trust your pack to care for them as we would our own, while you take this time to be with your alpha. I know it's not how we'd planned your first few days with the pups to go, but they are young and will be just fine in our care. It's only until your heat passes anyway."

"Did they have any nightmares," I asked Sy quietly. "They have them a lot, I wish I'd thought to warn you guys."

"Zane knew," Daniel said. "He slept in there with them, insisted on it, in fact. He thought it would be easier for them, since they are most comfortable with him right now."

I nodded my approval. "Good, I should have realized that he would have thought of that."

"Hey," I said suddenly, "were you as shocked as I was to see Tommy Collins' kid brother all grown up? Zane's such a good guy too. I wish I'd known about Tommy and their parents dying though, it broke my heart when Angie told me about that."

Daniel explained when Aries and Sy looked at me questioningly, "Zane's family was killed in a car crash last year. His older brother, Tommy, was Micah's best friend growing up. Zane used to try to follow us all around, but he was just a little guy, so we always ditched him."

"Damn. That's sucks, hon," Aries said, running a

comforting hand along my arm. "I'm sorry that you lost your friend."

"Yeah, it was rough to hear about," I said. "But I feel worse for Zane. Poor guy lost his whole family at once, you know?"

"I think we all know a little about that," my mate agreed with a sad smile. I felt a pang of remorse when I remembered that he'd lost his own grandmother from a car crash as well. "Remind me to thank him, when we finally get back. I appreciate him being there for the pups, especially sleeping in their room. I'm sure that they needed the comfort of having him there."

"He's a good kid." Daniel nodded. "I will let him know how much you both appreciate his help. And I'll let him be the one to tell Miss Sara that you're going to be away for a few days. You know, I wouldn't be surprised a bit to find out that little girl is an alpha herself."

Aries laughed, "Make sure you let her know that the *Daddy Guy* is being nice to her *Nutter Daddy*."

We all chuckled along with him at that one, my heart leaping for joy as I suddenly realized that Sara and Dylan were actually mine to keep now, because Aries and I had mated. Feeling my emotion through our bond, my mate clasped hands with me and smiled happily.

As if reading my mind, Daniel said, "Wow, she's going to freak out when they hear that you actually are going to be their dad now. That pup really adores you, Micah."

"Maybe it's for the best, you needing this time away from them," Sy said quietly. "When you two come back, you'll greet them as a combined parental unit, and that will definitely help them both accept Aries a lot faster."

Aries nodded and said honestly, "Not gonna lie, I will always hate that I have to get my own pups to accept me, but it's not their fault. Poor babies. I'm just so happy to actually have the chance though, you know? And the fact that I'm now mated to the infamous *Nutter Daddy* has got to get me some points with them, right?"

"Where the hell did that crazy name come from anyway," Sy asked.

I sighed, running a hand through my hair. "The day before we left, my friend Angie went to get Zane and his stuff. He needed a fresh start, and I needed help on the trip up here, so it was a perfect solution for both of us. She told him about the pups, and Aries, but neglected to tell him that the pups didn't know about their dad yet. I was going to let Aries tell them himself, you know?"

"Ah, and Zane let the cat out of the bag, so to speak?" Daniel said.

"Yeah, exactly. He innocently mentioned it, and Sara freaked out. I talked to her, but her response was that she didn't need *a nutter daddy*, because she had me. Angie and Zane kept teasing me and calling me the Nutter Daddy, and the name just kinda stuck. I never imagined that I would actually get to be their dad though," I admitted with a happy grin. "Getting Aries as my mate is a fantasy that I never would have had the imagination to dream up on my own, but to get those two beautiful angels too? That's just the complete package."

"Oh, gag me." Daniel chuckled, "I never thought I'd see the day that you turned into Mr. Mush, but look at you! Completely happy being shackled for life, not that I blame you for a second. Aries is a great guy," he nodded at my mate with a smirk, "and those pups are too cute for words. I'm just laughing because I really wouldn't have pictured you this way."

"Hey! Shackled! That reminds me!" Sy interjected,

"Aunt Kat sent the key!" But when he suddenly realized that we'd been sitting here uncuffed the whole time, Sy just shrugged and said, "Huh, I guess that's completely unnecessary, since I see that your lovely metal bracelets are already gone."

"Let me guess," Daniel said. "You shifted out?"

"Yeah," Aries giggled. "But we didn't think of it until this morning! Which reminds me..." He turned to Sy. "Would you mind bringing us a couple of shirts over at some point? Ours are kind of ripped to shreds."

"Sure," Sy agreed. "We'll do what we did when Alpha and Kai mated last year. We'll leave the basket of food on the porch, and knock to let you know it's there. You just remember to leave the empty one for us to swap out. When one of us delivers tomorrow's basket, there will be a couple shirts with it, okay?"

Aries nodded as I thought about what a perfect system that they had devised. Omegas were pretty clever, I realized, wondering how I'd ever thought of them as weak or dependent in the past.

Daniel and Sy finally made their goodbyes when Aries' cheeks started flushing and the pheromones of his heat began filling the air. We quickly saw them out and locked the door behind them, before racing back to the bedroom to get busy again. I was actually starting to really like this whole being mated thing, especially the fun parts where we got to be naked.

CHAPTER 10

ARIES

After four long days of being in heat finally ended, I was excited to be able to head back to the lodge. I would miss the long nights of thinking about nothing but the pleasure to be found at the receiving end of my alpha's knot, but it would be so good to finally be with my pups.

We walked back over, hand in hand, and entered the lodge. We had barely closed the door behind us when I heard Sara scream "*Nutter Daddy*!" as she came flying across the large area of the main sitting room to jump at Micah. He caught her easily, swinging her up in the air while she giggled merrily.

I froze, though, when a tiny voice softly said, "*Dada*." I looked down, and looking up at me was my son. He stood there with his pudgy little arms held up to me, wanting for me to pick him up. My eyes teared as I bent over and picked him up, cuddling him closely to my chest.

Turning at the sound of Micah's sharp intake of breath beside me, we exchanged a look of awed happiness while Zane came walking over.

"Did you hear that, Zaney? Dylan called Aries 'dada'," Micah said.

"Yeah, Sy's been showing them pictures of you on his phone," Zane said in explanation as he looked at me. "He's also been telling them a lot about you, and about how both Erin and Brianne are their half-sisters. Well, we just said sisters, but you know what I mean."

"Yes, wow, thank you!" I said, tears running down my cheeks now. Dylan reached out and touched my wet cheek questioningly, but I just nuzzled my face into his curls, inhaling his magical little boy scent. "And Zane, I want to thank you for taking such good care of them while we were gone. It was so much easier to be away, knowing that they were well cared for in our absence."

"No problem." He grinned. "You have awesome pups. We get along great. I just can't believe that I got to be here when Dylan spoke for the first time!"

"No kidding," said Micah, looking at me with a little smirk. "I'm not sure if I'm jealous that it wasn't me, or thrilled that it was you, to be honest."

"Oh, hush!" I chided. "You know that you're thrilled on my behalf. Besides, you've got your own arms full already." I glanced lovingly at my little Sara, who had her little arms wound tightly around her *Nutter Daddy*'s neck.

"Tell you what," Micah said, as he put his arm around my waist and pulled me closer. "Why don't we go outside and shift with the pups? We can all go play in the clearing across the way."

"Oh, yeah!" Zane enthused. "That's where we all go! I had promised the pups to take them today, so it's perfect if you guys do that with them instead."

"Have they eaten already?" I asked.

"Yep, we just finished breakfast a little while ago. They

should be good for as long as you want to have them out. They don't go down for naps until after lunch anyway. I mean, until you set your own routine, that is."

Smiling, I told him, "No, that's actually perfect. You did exactly what I would have done. And let me guess, bath after dinner then bed?"

"But, of course." Zane grinned back at me.

"See? Just like I would have done. Honestly, I don't know how I can ever thank you enough."

"Nah, it's cool. It kept me busy while I settled in anyway, and Sy was always right there if I needed him. We kinda tag teamed on the childcare, you know?"

I nodded, as Micah began pulling me toward the door impatiently. "I know exactly what you mean."

After he got me outside, Micah leaned over and placed a quick kiss on the tip of my nose and said, "Sorry, but you guys were getting cozy in there, and the pups and I want to play."

Sara was watching closely as we interacted, but so far hadn't said anything. I smiled at her, but let her stay with Micah, while I carried Dylan. She would come to me when she was ready. And I would be waiting with my arms wide open.

I laid down under the trees, panting with happy exhaustion from chasing butterflies with the pups. Watching now, as Micah gently played with them, I chuffed out a laugh and lowered my chin down to rest on my paws, while I watched over my family.

Family. I couldn't believe that I was mated now, and actually here with my very own pups and alpha, spending time together like a family should. Micah was the very last person on Earth that I would have chosen to mate, but somehow he was actually my perfect match.

I watched as the sun highlighted his dappled charcoal gray coat. The lighter streaks and shades that ran through it seemed to come alive when Micah moved around in the sunshine, muscles flexing as he romped with our pups.

He had Sara's roly-poly little gray pup body pinned down under one giant paw, while Dylan's tiny gray and white fluff of a wolf pup danced around them, yipping excitedly at his alpha parent for all he was worth. I suddenly wished for a human camera to capture this moment, it was that precious to me.

The Alpha-pair came walking through the trees a few minutes later. Kai came over and flopped down next me, while the Alpha went over and playfully growled at the pups. I shifted to human form while we watched as the two large alpha wolves played with my frisky little pups.

Kai shifted back a few minutes later, sitting next to me with our backs up against the large tree that we'd been lying under.

"It's so funny to see Alpha Jake play with my pups like this. I just hope it's not going to freak Micah out too much," I commented after a few minutes.

"It shouldn't," Kai said companionably. "Don't forget, but they did grow up together, you know? It's probably a much larger adjustment for your mate to think of Jake as the big Alpha, than it is to rough house with him."

"Hmm, that's true. I keep forgetting how much history these alphas around here have with each other. It's not like with us, who were pretty much forced together by circumstance, right?"

"Exactly. But then, we chose to be friends despite all that. That has its own charm, don't you think, Aries?"

"I think that if I hadn't had you other guys and Jenny to lean on back then, I probably wouldn't have survived my time in that cabin. Especially after my pups were taken from me."

"You know, it feels weird that I came along so late, that I didn't even know that you or Jenny had pups and that Fremont had taken them away. I almost feel left out, but I understand why you guys wouldn't have wanted to talk about it. I mean, Sy was pregnant when I met him, so I knew about Brianne from the start. It's Erin and your two that I feel left out of the loop about."

I reached over and took his hand. "Never feel that way, Kai. It's not that we didn't trust you, we just didn't talk about our pups at all. It was the only way that we could persevere. Jenny and Sy were there for a long time before I even told them about my pups. And the only reason I finally did was because they were pregnant and I wanted to warn them."

"Is it weird that I feel a little guilty that I wasn't assaulted too? It's like, I was just there long enough to make friends, and then have my big, bad alpha show up to save the day before things went south for me."

Looking over at Kai in shock, I nearly tripped over my tongue in my rush to respond. "Dude! Don't ever think that way! Thanks be to Fenris that your heat didn't come before Jake found us! Seriously, don't feel guilty about that for even one second. I'm grateful that you don't share in the shame that we've all had to deal with, and Luke and Ryan either. The fact that you three were spared is everything to me. I know that Jenny would have felt the same way if she were here, and I bet that Sy would tell you the same if you asked him."

Shaking his head, Kai said, "You're a good person, Aries. I used to wonder what you were thinking about, when you'd be all quiet and shit. Now, I think I know." He grinned as he turned to look at my tiny pups chasing the big wolves around the clearing.

Looking back at me, he said, "Seriously though, congratulations on your mating. I'm happy that Fenris has blessed you with a good alpha. And the fact that he and your pups already adore each other? That's everything, you know?"

"Yeah." I smiled softly. "I know. It really is everything, isn't it? I was thinking a few minutes ago that I wished we had a camera out here, to capture this moment of Micah and the pups. They're so cute together."

"I know," he said wistfully. "I can't wait until our pups are big enough to come out here and play. Erin should be able to soon enough, but the twins have a long ways yet to go."

"Be patient," I laughed. "Enjoy each stage, because the pups grow up fast enough, without us wishing them along faster."

"Patience sucks," he sulked. "But, you have a point. The twins are already twice the size that they were when they were born. It's going so fast!"

"Said every parent ever," Sy commented while sitting down to join us, with Brianne in his arms.

"Hey, buddy!" I greeted him, reaching out for Brianne. "I'm glad you came out, are you going to let this one start shifting outside soon and come out to play in the clearing with the bigger pups?"

The baby gurgled in my arms, making me smile indulgently as Sy said, "Hell, no. I'm going to keep my daughter a baby for as long as I can. Kai can push his pups out of the cradle all he wants, but this one? She will still be nursing in high school if she wants."

Kai and I both burst out laughing at that one. After we calmed down, I said, "You know that I'm going to remind you of that when she has all her teeth."

Sy rubbed his chest. "Don't remind me. Little brat has three already, and sometimes they scrape."

That had us giggling all over again, while Sy playfully pouted and grabbed his baby back away from me. The rest of the pack came and went, while we spent the peaceful morning hanging out in the clearing.

I knew it was lunch time when Sara started growling and trying to nip at every tail that crossed her path. Zane was right, I mused with a grin. The *hanger* really was strong with that one.

Once Micah and I rounded up the pups and got them home, lunch went quickly. Turns out, pups tend to get really hungry if you wear them out by letting them play outside in the sunshine. Good to know.

Doc Ollie came up during lunch, and quietly asked if he could talk to us. I glanced at Micah's sheepish expression, and invited Doc to join us.

"I wanted to apologize for offending you the other evening. I truly meant no harm," he stated politely, in that formal way that I'd noticed the bears all shared.

"Naw, Doc. That was just me being an overprotective grump. I'm new at this dad business, you know? But my mate is right, if there is something that we need to know about with our pup, we should definitely have you look at her."

I nodded my agreement, as I took a bite that I almost choked on a moment later, when Doc spoke again.

"Good, good. Well, why don't you bring her by this afternoon, and I'll take a look at her? That would be a good time to check you out too, Aries. To make sure that your body is ready for this new pregnancy."

While I was trying not to choke, Micah asked blankly, "Pregnancy? What pregnancy? We're not trying for any pups yet."

Doc chuckled and said, "Good, don't worry about trying then, because you've already succeeded. Your mate here is pregnant, I can smell the change in his scent."

"I didn't notice any change," Micah said, looking at me curiously.

"You wouldn't have, not yet anyway. As I've explained to the Alpha in the past, we bears have a much higher sense of smell than you wolves do. Perhaps that is why so many us choose careers in the medical fields? Ah, a thought to ponder later, I suppose. But, nevertheless, Aries is definitely pregnant. I'll need to look him over and give him some prenatal vitamins to take."

"Thanks, Doc," I said happily. "We'll be by later, after the little guys have their nap."

Doc Ollie nodded absently in his own odd way, and wandered off again. I looked over at my mate, who seemed to be frozen in shock at the moment.

"Gee, alpha. What's up with that face? I thought that they taught you in school all about what could happen if you popped a knot with an omega in heat," I teased.

He looked at me then, his eyes full of wonder. "I know, I know. It's just that, I never really thought I'd have a pup of my own, and now I get to have three."

My heart burst when he said that, loving that he considered my pups to be as much his own as this new baby would be. My mate was truly one of a kind. I guess that maybe Fenris did know what he was doing when he paired us.

After lunch, we took the pups up to their room and settled them into their beds. They were both asleep before I could make it even halfway through the book I'd chosen to read for them.

We tucked them in, and then Micah took my hand, leading me quietly into our adjoining room and silently closing the door behind us. While we'd been shacked up in the cabin, riding my heat out, our thoughtful pack-mates had brought Micah's things to my room, making it ours now.

"Nice digs," Micah said, reading my thoughts through our open connection.

"I was assigned this room right before you arrived. I've never even slept in here yet, so it's new to us both, honestly."

"Really? That's pretty cool," Micah said with a smile, laying down on the bed and pulling me down beside him. "I guess that means we can break it in together then."

"I don't how much breaking in that you think we can do with our little guys asleep in the next room."

Wiggling his eyebrows, he rolled over on top of me and whispered in my ear, "Why do you think that I shut the door? You just have to be very, very quiet. None of those loud porn-star moans that you're so famous for, babe."

I smacked his arm and bit my lip to hold in a giggle.

Thrusting his already hard cock against me, I groaned at the delicious friction through my jeans.

"See what I mean?" he whispered, while thrusting harder against me, "There you go already with the porn-star moans."

After we fooled around for awhile, I ended falling asleep in Micah's arms. I woke up to the sound of his voice in the next room, and quickly got up and pulled my clothes back on so that I could join them.

After Doc Ollie was done examining our completely irritated daughter, he rolled back on his stool and suggested that I let her go play in the other room where Luke was watching Dylan. Luke was Doc's office assistant, and he was kind enough to watch the little ones that came in with their parents when the need arose.

Doc had checked Dylan out first and found him to be in perfect condition. Apparently his non-verbal behavior was either from trauma, or else he was just a late bloomer. We would watch him, and encourage him to talk. If that didn't work, then Doc told us that he could refer us to a child psychologist that lived over in the neighboring bear den.

Sara went willingly with Micah, and once he came back alone, Doc told us what was going on.

"Your daughter is tongue tied, to put it in layman's terms. It is a simple procedure to fix this for her, and you will find her speech improving dramatically afterwards. She may need to see a speech therapist to relearn how to make sounds, but then again, she is young enough that it could just correct itself."

"What do you mean by tongue-tied, Doc?" Micah asked curiously.

"Basically, the little piece of tissue that connects her tongue to the base of the mouth is too short, or tight you might say, for young Sara to speak properly."

"And how would you go about correcting this," Micah asked before I could.

"It's a simple little clip actually. I will numb the area

first with a topical anesthetic, and snip-snip, the problem is fixed. Since she's a shifter, she will most likely be healed before her next meal. It's simpler for us than for humans, is it not? But I digress. My point is that this is quite simply fixed, and I can do it right here in the clinic. It will fix her right up, I can almost promise you."

"Can we be there, while you do it?" I asked hesitantly.

"Yes, but only you. The alpha dad can be here until she's comfortable, but then he must leave. I cannot risk inciting the protective alpha instincts that would cause you to try and fight me. This would create harm for the child if my hand should slip."

Doc looked sternly at Micah as he said this. Micah simply nodded his acceptance, and we moved on.

"How soon can we do it, Doc?" I asked, knowing already that we would agree to do it.

"Honestly? I can do it right now and examine you another day, so that you don't have to bring the girl back a second time." Doc chuckled for moment. "The young alpha really did not care for being examined, did she?"

"You think that Sara's an alpha?" I asked curiously. We had joked about it, but I hadn't taken it seriously.

"How could that dominant child be anything else? Her alpha pheromones are off the charts for a girl her age. Again, it's all in the bear nose," he said as he tapped a finger to the side of his nose. "Trust me, you will smell it clearly once she reaches puberty. But for now, you can take my word for it."

"And my son?" I asked, "what is his classification?"

"Ah, that sweet soul is an omega like you, my dear. Through and through."

"Wow," Micah said. "I guess we'll have to watch how much we let Sara boss him around then. We'll want to make sure that our boy doesn't grow up being used to getting bossed around by alphas everywhere he goes."

I looked at my mate, and smiled contentedly. I loved how much he adored my children, and thought of their every need. It would be funny, seeing how his ideas regarding omegas might continue to expand, now that he knew for sure that our son was one too.

"Okay, Doc," I said. "Let's go ahead and take care of Sara first. I can come back tomorrow, or later in the week for my own examination."

"I'll get Sara now," Micah said firmly, "but we will definitely be back in here tomorrow to have Aries examined, if you have time."

Doc smiled knowingly at my alpha mate, as I rolled my eyes with a grin. After Micah brought Sara back in, Doc had her lay back on the exam table, while I held her head. Nutter Daddy explained that this was something that she needed to have done, and that *Daddy Guy,* as she'd taken to calling me, was going to help the doctor while he checked on Dylan.

As always, she willingly did as my mate asked, and he stepped outside so that Doc could do his thing. Sara stoically laid there while Doc numbed her mouth, before doing the quick procedure a few minutes later. Afterwards, she allowed me to hold her while I carried her out to where Micah and Dylan were waiting. It was a small victory, but I treasured every second that I got to hold her little body against my chest.

CHAPTER 11
MICAH

"Should you still be this sick, sweetheart?" I asked Aries while he knelt in front of the toilet, after purging yet another meal. "I thought that morning sickness was supposed to pass after the first month, and you're almost into the final stretch now! At this rate, the baby will be born before the sickness passes."

Aries glared up at me and said, "I'm well aware of that, Micah. Trust me, I'm aware. Doc said that it's common for some people to be sick the entire three months of gestation. It looks like I was just one of those lucky fucking people."

"Well, I don't like it. Were you sick like this with your other pregnancies?"

"Hell, no. I was barely sick with Sara at all, and with Dylan, it passed after a couple weeks. This is totally new for me, and it fucking sucks," he growled. "Now, can we just quit talking about it, please?"

I bit back any further comments, not wanting to piss my poor mate off any more than he already was. "How about I go and get you a cup of that mint tea, and some soda crackers then? Those usually seem to help, don't they?"

With a long-suffering sigh, Aries nodded his head as I helped him up to brush his teeth. After planting a quick kiss on his temple, I went downstairs to find his tea and crackers.

I walked into the kitchen to find Sy already plating a tray with a small pot of mint tea, and an array of crackers. He looked up at me, and smiled knowingly.

"Did you put your foot in it again?"

Nodding, I said, "I just don't understand why it upsets him that I care."

"It's not that you care, my friend. It's because you hover," Sy explained. "I know that you can't help it, it's just part of the whole protective alpha thing. But you need to understand that we omegas need space sometimes, especially when we're pregnant and totally miserable."

I nodded glumly, wishing that I could do something to cheer my mate up and take away his suffering.

"Listen, why don't you go play with your pups, and I'll take this up to Aries and keep him company for you this morning."

"You'll make sure that he rests and doesn't strain himself?"

Sy rolled his eyes, and said, "I'll make sure that he's comforted, and gets some food down. He doesn't need to rest, he needs to not puke. Simple as that. Now go get your monsters, and I'll tend to your mate, okay?"

I reluctantly let him go by with the tray, pushing back my urge to go and coddle Aries, knowing full well that it would only piss him off if I tried.

"He's sick again, huh?" Jake asked knowingly as he walked in the kitchen.

"Yeah, and he gets mad every time that I try to talk to him about it."

"Get used to it, buddy. This is pure omega territory, and

there's nothing you can do but ride it out. You think this shit is rough? Wait until he's in delivery and they kick you out of the room."

"They wouldn't dare!" I bared my teeth at the thought of being kept away.

"Exactly. That right there is why they will. That whole protective, cave-man shit that we alphas do? That's why you won't be allowed near the delivery area. Apparently, we couldn't deal with seeing our mate go through something like that. That's what they told me, anyway."

"But you're the Alpha! How could you be kept away from your own mate's delivery room?"

"When it comes to this kind of thing, rank doesn't matter. If you're not the doctor or another omega, you're not welcome in there. It's just how it is. But chin up, it will all be over in the next few days. After that, you'll get your mate back. And a precious new pup as a bonus. Trust me, it will be okay," Jake assured me.

"I guess. I'm just gonna go take the pups out to play, get us all outside for awhile in the sunshine."

"Now that's a plan! Take the little guys and run around with them, they'll get your mind off your mate worries for a few."

"You make it sound easy, Jake."

"I know. But trust me. I was messed up the whole time Kai was pregnant too. It's easier for me, because I'm on the other side of it now. If he ever catches again, you'll see a whole other side of me, and it won't be nearly as calm as I'm advising you to be," he laughed.

"Excuse me? If Kai ever catches what?" the spunky little alpha-mate said, as he came walking in with Erin on his hip. "You'd better be talking about me catching a human cold, because that's far more likely since I've got three pups right now and only two hands."

Jake laughed. "I was just talking Micah down, he's stressed about Aries. I was telling him that he didn't see me when you were pregnant, but if you ever caught again, he'd see a whole other side of me."

Kai rolled his eyes dramatically. "Let me put it out there like this, Micah. His Aunt Kat had to forcibly drag him out of my delivery room. Seriously. The dude didn't know how to back off."

I grinned, loving how the two of them meshed so well together. It was good to see my old friend settled down so happily.

"Seriously though, Micah," Kai said, "Don't worry about Aries. He's okay, and if he wasn't, Doc would have said something. He's really good about this stuff. I know it's hard, especially with how sick poor Aries has been through this whole pregnancy, but don't worry. He'll be okay. He's still getting enough nourishment, whether it feels like that to you or not. Just tell your wolf to shut the hell up, and let Aries do his thing. Trust me."

I nodded, and asked Jake, "Any other helpful tips before I go shift with my pups?"

"Yeah," he said with a smirk, "make sure you get laid in the next day or two because you'll have to wait awhile after he delivers. And that's if he'll even let you touch him again."

"Oh, bullshit. Because that's what a nauseous omega with a watermelon in his gut really wants? To get laid? Seriously, Jake. Did your parents drop you on your head as a pup?" Kai glared playfully at his mate with a quirked brow.

"I dunno," Jake said with a smirk, "I seem to remember another omega that really want to get some of that magical knot action right up until delivery."

"I'm done. I give up. Micah, ignore my mate. He's an idiot." Kai stalked out of the room muttering under his breath, while Jake laughed his ass off.

"You know you're gonna pay for that later, right?" I asked him with a grin.

"Oh, trust me, I'm counting on it!" Jake chuckled wickedly, as I shook my head and walked away smiling.

The pups and I played together for the rest of the morning out in the peaceful sunshine along with Luke and Ryan, the young omega teens that were members of our pack.

Sara loved playing with them. They were much smaller than my wolf, so she could tackle them easier. Ryan usually let her take him down, but Luke would challenge her and make her work for it.

I let them tussle, while I helped Dylan hunt a mouse. I figured that it was never too early to teach my omega son how to take care of himself in the wild. At his age, it would probably scare him more than the mouse, if he actually caught the damn thing. But it was good to teach him how to track its scent.

As it got closer to lunch time, I chuffed out a command to Sara before I lifted the little ball of fluff at my feet by the scruff of his neck to carry across the parking area, to the porch of the lodge where we all liked to shift and change.

I grinned when I saw Luke pick Sara up the same way, as he and Ryan followed me over. Once we were all shifted and dressed, I took the pups in for their lunch, with the two brothers still following along behind me. They ended up joining us, along with a couple of my alpha friends, Maxx and Owen.

"So, what have you guys been up to? I've barely seen either of you since I moved here. What's up with that?"

"We've been hanging out with the bears a lot. They've been teaching us some cool hunting techniques," Maxx explained.

"I was just wondering. I've seen you guys in passing, but that's about it."

"Yeah, well, you've also been kinda busy with the whole mate and babies thing yourself," Owen chimed in.

"That's true," I had to admit. "Hey, do you guys know a bear named Karl?"

"Oh, yeah," said Owen. "He's a really nice guy! How do you know him?"

"When I drove in a few months ago, we had a flat about five miles out. Karl showed up out of nowhere and insisted I let him change it for me. I promised him a lager one of these days, I should probably see about paying up for that at some point."

"Dude," Maxx said. "You do NOT want to go drinking with the bears! Those fu—umm, fun guys will drink you under the table." He caught himself mid-swear when he noticed Sara listening intently from her spot over at the kids' table.

I chuckled at the faint blush that was crawling up his neck. "What's wrong, Maxi-pad? You scared of getting in trouble with my pup?"

"Shi—I mean, shoot. That girl is more alpha that all of us, I'm pretty sure. You should have heard her lecturing us yesterday, because we were rough housing in the clearing while her little brother was nearby. If she wasn't so tiny, I would be scared of her."

"Pfft. Like you're not anyway." Owen grinned. He looked over at me and winked before he continued: "Maxx can't handle getting schooled by a pup. You should have seen him nearly piss himself when she stood there with her hands on her little hips, yelling up at us. It was hysterical."

We joked around some more, until I noticed Dylan rubbing his eyes. "Time for me to go, guys," I told my friends, "As much as I'd like to stay longer and hear about how my tiny daughter scared the piss out of Maxx, even tough little soldiers like her need their afternoon naps."

Motioning for the kids to come on, I cupped a hand over Luke's shoulder and thanked him and his brother for helping me out with the pups this morning.

"It was a pleasure," Luke said shyly. "I like your pups. They're sweeties."

Maxx snorted at that, which had Owen choking out a laugh. I grinned in amusement as I bent down and picked up Dylan, reaching for Sara's hand.

"Say goodbye to everyone, Sara."

"Bye, everybody. I see you waiter."

The guys looked confused, so I echoed her and said, "Yeah, see you guys *later*."

Smiling proudly at how much clearer her speech was getting, though, I led her out of the dining area and headed for our rooms upstairs. As much as I'd hated having to let Doc snip, clip, or whatever the hell it was he'd done to her, it really had been for the best.

The downside was that the clearer her speech became, the more her natural alpha bossiness started to show as her confidence grew. Not that I minded it all that much, I was proud to have a feisty girl that had no problems facing down huge alpha men.

If she wasn't afraid of them at this age, I figured that maybe I wouldn't have to worry as much when she was a teenager and the other kids started sniffing around her. Thank Fenris that was a good ten years off, though.

Once I had them both tucked in for their naps, I poked my head into our room to check on my mate. He was laying in bed reading, when I sheepishly caught his eye. Aries raised a brow, but merely patted the mattress next to him.

I walked over and pulled off my shoes before laying down beside my mate and pulling him over to spoon up against me. He was wearing just a pair of old sweats, with no shirt on.

Apparently pregnancy made him run hot, which was awesome for me, because that meant that I got to see his muscular chest and cute baby belly as much as I wanted. It was hard to keep my eyes and hands off him, to be honest.

"How come you're all alone in here? I thought for sure that one of your friends would be hanging out and bashing all of us stupid alphas about now."

"Oh, hush. I sent them away because I knew it was about nap time, and I was hoping for some cuddle time with the Nutter Daddy."

"I hope she doesn't stop calling me that any time soon. Have you noticed how much clearer her speech is getting?"

"Yeah, it's amazing. I don't think we'll need to worry about the speech specialist recommendation from Doc, if she keeps improving so much. I try to correct her whenever she says a sound wrong, even though I hate to do it."

I cuddled him closer, kissing his shoulder as I wrapped my arm around his waist and cradled his big baby belly with my hand. "You just don't want to be the bad guy. Admit it, you'd rather make me be the one to piss her off, while you get to be the sweet little *Daddy Guy*."

He giggled. "Well she finally accepts me, somewhat

anyway. I don't want to screw that up, you know? But at the same time, I want to do right by her."

"Yeah. I get it, babe. Parenthood sucks. You know what else sucks?"

"I'm hoping you'll say that you do, because I can't seem to find my own dick these days, let alone properly stroke it when you're not around to help me with it."

I lowered my hand to cup his crotch, kissing his neck as I whispered, "I'm always happy to give you a hand." *Kiss.* "Or a mouth." *Kiss.* "Or even a knot." I sucked over his claim mark then, making him squirm as he pushed his ass back and rubbed up against my crotch. "And if I'm not around, just holler. I'll come running every time, if it means that I get to be handsy with my mate."

"Micah. You're starting to piss me off, babe."

I jerked my head up, alarmed. "What did I do? I can fix it. Just tell me."

Pushing his ass up firmly against my stiff cock, Aries said, "It's nothing you did, it's what you aren't doing."

"What do I need to be doing?"

"Me."

Oh. *OH*! "Now that I can definitely fix." I pushed the elastic waist of his sweatpants down, and reached my hand inside to stroke his length. "What would you like me to do first, sweet-cheeks? You're the boss today, so name it."

I watched the blush coloring his cheek as I leaned over him, kissing his jaw and licking my way down along his neck.

"How long do you think we have?"

"The pups are worn out. I had them outside playing all morning. So at least another hour and a half, I would guess."

"Lock the doors?"

"You got it." I gave his cock one quick tug and kissed his

claim mark, then got up and quickly went over to lock both the adjoining door to the pups' room, and the door to the hall.

Once I knew that we had complete privacy, I stripped off my shirt. I slowly stalked towards my mate, who was eyeing my body like a slab of raw meat while my clothes quickly went flying.

I went back over to the bed and pulled his pants off with one firm yank, before crawling back up and dropping down carefully onto the bed next to him. Aries was laying on his side facing away from me, while arching his back and pushing that ass towards me.

"Tell me what you want, baby." I ran a finger slowly down his spine and across the crack of his tight, juicy ass.

"I want your knot, and I don't want to waste any time with foreplay. I just want you to take me hard, rough, and fast."

"Fuck, sweet-cheeks. Are you even hearing yourself right now?"

He turned his head to look back at me over his shoulder, with a sexy little smirk on his pouty lips. "Do you have a problem with that, mate?"

"Yeah. Because you're gonna make me nut before I even get my dick wet."

"Then get in there, big boy. Tick-tock, time's a wasting." Reaching down, the brat grabbed his ass cheek, spreading it open just enough for me to see the slick already shining from his hole.

I pushed up against him, rubbing my hard cock between his cheeks while I bent my head down and nipped at his claim mark. "So. You said no foreplay and no teasing?"

"None of that shit right now. Just fuck me, alpha."

Reaching down to grab my cock, I kept nipping and

licking his mark while I lined myself up with his hole. I reached both hands up and grabbed his hips, thrusting right past his rim and sinking inside of him with one quick pump of my hips. I paused for a moment to let us both adjust, and waited for his nod to continue.

"I said to take me, alpha. Now, quit waiting and fuck me already. What's a man gotta do to get laid around here?"

Chuckling, I started thrusting slow and steady, until I got my rhythm going, then I wrapped my arm around around his waist over the baby belly. Pulling him against me and locking him in place with my right arm while my left hand was firmly grabbing his hip from underneath, I pounded into him. He writhed and panted, as I quickly picked up speed.

The only sounds in the room were those of our sweaty flesh slapping together and our quiet pants and gasps. My knot was already swelling up, and I was having a harder time pulling out with each downstroke.

Moving my hand from his waist, I pushed his shoulders forward, holding his upper body away from me with the flat of my hand as I arched backwards and thrust forward with shallow rocks of my hips, now that my knot was truly good and stuck inside his rim.

"Need... help?" I gasped out, wondering if he needed a hand on his cock to tip him over the edge.

Shaking his head furiously, he panted, "Just. Don't. Stop."

My left hand gripped his hip tighter, while I still kept his shoulders pushed forward with my right hand. I tilted my hips up slightly to better hit that little bundle of nerves inside his ass, while I kept humping into him with a furious pace.

"Yes, alpha, yes!" he gasped out in a whisper, his scent

filling the room as ropes of cum started squirting out and shooting over the mattress in front of him.

I rode that ass hard through his orgasm. It was his channel clenching around my cock that finally pushed me over the edge. I dipped my head to rest my forehead between his sweaty shoulder blades, while my own release filled his ass with hot liquid as I climaxed.

"Holy shit, babe," my mate panted, as I came back to reality after a few moments of sheer bliss. "That was fucking hot."

Pulling his shoulders up against my chest, I wriggled around settling us in, until we were both comfortable while we waited for my knot to go back down.

"Yeah, it was! But I didn't hurt you, did I? That wasn't too rough?"

"No, baby. Doc said that this was perfectly safe, remember?"

"I know, I just, well, damn. That was some pretty hard pounding that you wanted there."

"Yeah, I've been really horny lately. I had a window here where I didn't feel like puking, so I wanted to take advantage of it. And you. I always want to take advantage of you." He giggled then, making me grin at what an adorably sexy man that I had for a mate.

This was my favorite part of sex now. Well, aside from the actual fucking. I got to cuddle my man and have him all to myself, for as long as it took for my knot to relax. These times of intimacy were precious to me, I couldn't even fathom how I ever could have lived without this man at my side.

"Am I allowed to ask how much you puked after I left earlier?"

Aries sighed. "I'm sorry, Micah. I know how much you

care about me, and that you worry. Not because of the whole alpha thing, but because you really love me. I get that. I just hate talking about being sick, especially right after I get done with a bout of it. You caught me at a bad time this morning, babe. I hate myself when I get all prickly with you." He swiped at tears and muttered something about 'damn hormones' under his breath.

"Hey, now." I wrapped my arm that was under him around his waist, while I stroked his belly with my top hand. "Don't feel bad, baby. I know this has been a shitty pregnancy for you, and I hate seeing you beat yourself up for being honest with me. If I'm being a douche-bag, just tell me. I can take it."

"No, it's not you. Well, sometimes it is? But you can't help it. I just hate that I'm feeling like this, when this should be a happy time for us! We're having a baby together, our own pup. And I can't even enjoy the process."

"First of all, fuck the process. Our happy time will be when we get to meet the little one. That's the whole point of pregnancies, right? To get a healthy baby? Everything else is just life. Second of all, we have our own pups already. Sara and Dylan are every bit as much mine as they are yours. I thought you knew that, Aries. This baby is an addition to our family, but it's not any more important than the little guys that we already have, okay?"

"Oh, fuck. You're gonna make me cry again," Aries said as he poked an elbow back against my gut.

"Oof. Watch those bony elbows, omega. Or else," I growled playfully in his ear, hugging him closer against me as I inhaled his scent.

"Or else what?"

"Or else I'm gonna have to bend you over and redden that little smart ass."

"Good luck with that one, when I've got a beach ball sticking out of the front of me."

"Oh, I have a long memory, babe. I'll wait until I can stretch you over my lap again, and then I'll paddle your butt until it glows."

"Then what will you do?"

"Then? Why, that's when I get to kiss it and make it all better," I said as I nipped his earlobe.

"I love you, Micah."

"I love you, too, Aries. Now let's take a nap. My mate wore me out."

"That sounds good. I like that plan."

"Me too, babe."

We ended up taking a long nap. When we woke up, I pulled on my clothes and helped my mate get into his own pants again, before I went to see about our pups. I felt like a shitty parent, taking a nap while my pups were off on their own.

I opened the adjoining door though, and found Sy sitting there playing with blocks with my pups and little Brianne. Leaning against the door frame, I smiled fondly as I watched while Sara patiently showed Brianne how to stack the blocks properly.

The kid was a true alpha, through and through. Sy's baby was only about ten months old, so she had no interest in doing anything other than gnawing on the blocks at this point, but Sara seemed determined to help her half-sister learn to stack them anyway.

"Hey, there. Did you guys have a nice nap?" Sy smirked up at me, with knowing eyes.

"Yeah. We didn't mean to sleep so long. I'm sorry if we put you out."

"No, it's okay. Sara came and found me when you guys

didn't answer her knock," he answered kindly. "Did Aries finally get some rest?"

"Yeah, he was out like a log. He's awake now, if you wanna go in."

Sy nodded and got up from the floor. I saw him start to hesitate, looking at Brianne, but I quickly reassured him. "Go ahead, I'll watch your little one, you go hang out with Aries. He's getting sick of being stuck in bed."

"I'm right here, you know. You don't need to talk about me like I'm not in the same damned room," Aries said, his voice carrying across the room from the bed behind me. I looked over my shoulder at him and grinned, as Sy pushed past me and went to curl up at the foot our bed and visit with my mate.

"You want me to shut the door, so you two can have some privacy?"

"No, thanks, baby. But I want the pups to be able to come see me if they want to."

"Alright, well, the offer is there." I walked into the kids room and got down on the floor to play with my pups. While Sara had me helping her with the tower, I noticed Dylan get up and pick up a book, before he carried it into our bedroom to have his daddy read it to him. I smiled, knowing how much that would mean to my mate. I focused on stacking the blocks with Sara, while Brianne busily chewed on one and watched us play.

Sometime during the night, Aries woke me and insistently urged me to get up and go get the Doc. I blinked my eyes at him, not understanding what was happening when I slowly realized that our bed was soaked. His water had broken while we slept.

Oh, shit! I jumped as I realized that *his water had broken*! I started to run for the door, when I heard Aries dryly comment behind me: "Babe, you might wanna consider putting some pants on before you go knocking at another man's door in the middle of the night."

Right. Pants. I looked around the room in confusion, temporarily forgetting where I could locate pants. Aries rolled his eyes and merely pointed at the pile of clothes on the floor that I'd shucked off earlier when I went to bed.

Embarrassed, I went over and pulled on my pants. I threw the shirt over my head and was struggling with the arms, while I fumbled with the doorknob and then went down the hall to knock on Doc's door.

While I waited for him to answer, the door of the room next to his popped open, and Jake's aunt stepped out. "Let me guess, your mate is finally ready to deliver?"

I nodded my head as Doc opened his door, his medical bag in hand.

"It is that time?" he asked me calmly, with a raised brow.

"Yeah, Aries' water broke while we were sleeping."

"Okay. You go downstairs. I will come to find you when the baby is here."

I nodded reluctantly, firmly aware of his 'no alphas' rule for the delivery. I watched him walk down to our room, my fists clenched at the inability to be there for my mate right now.

A small hand gripped my arm, and I heard Aunt Kat say, "Come with me. We'll just go downstairs and have ourselves a nice cup of tea. I can tell you all about my books, and the various research that goes into writing them. You wouldn't believe the interesting gadgets that I have picked up since I started writing my stories!"

The door across the hall flew open, and Kai came rushing out. "No! Don't you dare scare him right now, Auntie! Jake's coming out to keep him company. I'm gonna go get Sy and see what we can do to help Doc with Aries."

"Oh, nonsense! A big, strapping alpha like Micah here isn't going to be scared of a little old beta wolf like me! Honestly, I don't know where you boys get your ideas."

Jake came strolling out, sending Kai off with a swat to his butt as he flashed me a lazy grin and said, "It's okay, man. Just don't ask her about cock cages and you'll be just fine with my aunt here."

"Cock... what now?" I asked reluctantly, after I found my tongue.

"Oh, they're the neatest little devices! I actually have one in my office if you want to see it!"

"No!" Jake said quickly, as he put an arm around his aunt and steered her toward the stairs. "Come on, Micah. I have a deck of cards in my office. I'll grab them for us, and Aunt Kat can teach you some slap jack, instead of scaring you into never wanting to have sex again."

I looked back longingly over my shoulder towards the open door to our room, but I followed my Alpha and his kooky little aunt down the stairs instead. As much I wanted to be with my mate, I knew that I needed to do as I was asked and just let him do his thing, while I made myself scarce for the duration.

Jake and his aunt stayed with me all night, playing cards and keeping me calm, while Aries delivered the newest member of our little family. After the first hour, I was cracking up from Aunt Kat's jokes and innuendos. Jake kept warning me not to encourage her, but I seriously thought that the little crackerjack was probably the most awesome old lady that I'd ever met.

As I saw the sky lighting with the sunrise of a new day, Kai came bouncing into the doorway and chirped happily, "Come back upstairs now, Micah. It's time to meet your new pup."

Dropping my cards, I jumped from the table and dashed through the doorway, stopping long enough to give Kai a quick hug. I could hear Jake chuckling behind me as I shouted "Thanks!" to the room behind me before dashing up the stairs and down the hall to our room.

I skidded to a stop when I came through our door and saw Aries sitting back against a mound of pillows, cradling a newborn babe. He looked up at me with a beatific smile, as I went around the bed to crawl up beside them. My eyes were blurry with tears as I looked down at the precious angel in my mate's arms.

"Hey, Nutter Daddy," Aries said softly. "Meet Linus, our newest son."

I reached out to stroke a trembling finger down Linus' petal soft cheek, tears freely falling now. "Hey there, Linus. I'm your Papa. It's about time you came out to meet us."

Aries snorted. "Good luck with that Papa shit. Sara's never gonna let that fly. I'm pretty sure she's sticking with the whole Nutter Daddy thing permanently. Especially if she ever finds out how much it bugs you."

I chuckled through my happy tears, leaning in to press a kiss to my mate's lips. "Honestly? Our pups can call me anything they want, as long as they're here and remember to call me something, you know?"

"I'm pretty sure I'm the poster child for knowing what it feels like to want your pups to know you and remember you."

"Aries, you're one omega that I'll always remember."

"I know, babe. I know."

We kissed again, before breaking apart to smile down at our pup. It was amazing how much I already loved the little guy who had just joined our family. My amazing little Linus.

The adjoining door flew open sometime later, as our older pups came flying in and hopped up on the bed.

"See, Dywan! I towed you that I could smell the baby!" Sara announced triumphantly as Dylan crawled up over our legs and snuggled in between us to see his new little brother.

"Ba-bee?" Dylan asked in his hesitant little voice. He still only spoke a few words, but each one was precious to hear him say.

"Yeah, buddy." I grinned, reaching down to tickle his belly. "This is Linus, he's your new baby brother."

Sara climbed up onto my lap, peering across Dylan's head to see Linus better. "Daddy Guy, I towed you to give us a sister. Didn't Nutter Daddy say to you that I wanted a sister?"

Aries and I smiled at each other, Sara still hadn't mastered her 'L' or 'TH' sounds, but her speech was much more intelligible now. Demanding, but intelligible.

"Sorry, sweetie," Aries said patiently. "Fenris is the one who decides when we get girl or boy pups. Not me or Nutter Daddy."

"Okay, Daddy Guy." Sara thought for a minute. "Den you just have to get us a nutter baby, okay?"

I choked back a laugh as Aries' face went pale for a

minute, while he looked over at Sara in horror before I finally said, "Sara, angel. Let's just enjoy Linus for awhile before we ask Daddy Guy to have another baby, okay? Let's just have one baby at a time."

"Besides," Sy said quietly, as he came in the room carrying Brianne. "You already have two little sisters, Sara. Remember? Erin and Brianne are both your sisters, aren't they?"

To my mate's visible relief, Sara bought that, for now. She nodded happily at Sy and then changed the subject to start badgering Aries to let her hold the baby. He looked over at me and rolled his eyes before saying, "Yeah, I think that we're totally good with the family we have right now. Don't you agree, alpha?"

I wrapped my arm around Aries' shoulders, leaning in to kiss his claim mark before pulling him over to lean against my shoulder. I wrapped my other arm around Sara, letting my hand rest on Dylan's soft head full of curls where he sat wedged in between my legs now. "Yes, omega of mine. We're definitely good with the family we have now. In fact, I'd say that we're the perfect family."

fin

What happens when your fated mate is also your natural predator?

Get your FREE copy of The Rabbit Chase:

https://dl.bookfunnel.com/vfk1sa9pu3

Would you like to get updates about future releases? Sign up for my newsletter:

The Hawke's Nest
http://eepurl.com/cWBy9T

Twitter:
https://twitter.com/SusiHawkeAuthor

Facebook:
https://www.facebook.com/SusiHawkeAuthor

ALSO BY SUSI HAWKE

Northern Lodge Pack Series

Omega Stolen: Book 1

Omega Remembered: Book 2

Omega Healed: Book 3

Omega Shared: Book 4

Omega Matured: Book 5

Omega Accepted: Book 6

Omega Grown: Book 7

Northern Pines Den Series

Alpha's Heart: Book 1

Alpha's Mates: Book 2

Alpha's Strength: Book 3

Alpha's Wolf: Book 4

Alpha's Redemption: Book 5

Alpha's Solstice: Book 6

Blood Legacy Chronicles

Alpha's Dream: Book 1

Non-Shifter Contemporary Mpreg

Pumpkin Spiced Omega: The Hollydale Omegas - Book 1

Cinnamon Spiced Omega: The Hollydale Omegas - Book 2

Peppermint Spiced Omega: The Hollydale Omegas - Book 3

Made in the USA
Las Vegas, NV
27 March 2022